Betrayed!

"We are under no obligation to provide further for you, madam," said the king coldly. "The prince of Wales repudiated the marriage agreement before his fourteenth birthday. Your support became entirely your father's duty, not ours. Anything we give you is merely Christian alms. Be grateful for what you have." He turned away, waving his hand in dismissal.

So it was true! Henry had broken his promise to me!

"Such words are not worthy of your Grace!" I cried. Nearly blinded by tears of humiliation, I made the necessary obeisances and fled from his chamber.

Patience, Princess Catherine

A YOUNG ROYALS BOOK

Patience, Princess Catherine

Carolyn Meyer

Harcourt, Inc.

Orlando Austin New York San Diego London

Copyright © 2004 by Carolyn Meyer

www.HarcourtBooks.com

First Harcourt paperback edition 2005
First published 2004

The Library of Congress has cataloged the hardcover edition as follows:
Meyer, Carolyn, 1935–
Patience, Princess Catherine/Carolyn Meyer.
p. cm.
Summary: In 1501 fifteen-year-old Catherine of Aragon arrives in England to marry Arthur, the eldest son of King Henry VII, but soon finds her expectations of a happy settled life radically changed when Arthur unexpectedly dies and her future becomes the subject of a bitter dispute between the kingdoms of England and Spain. 1. Catherine, of Aragon, Queen, consort of Henry VIII, King of England, 1485–1536—Juvenile fiction.
[1. Catherine, of Aragon, Queen, consort of Henry VIII, King of England, 1485–1536—Fiction. 2. Kings, queens, rulers, etc.—Fiction.
3. Great Britain—History—Henry VII, 1485–1509—Fiction.] I. Title.
PZ7.M5685Pat 2004
[Fic]—dc22   2003017611
ISBN 978-0-15-216544-4
ISBN 978-0-15-205447-2 pb

Text set in Granjon
Designed by Lydia D'moch

E G I J H F D

Printed in the United States of America

For Mary R. Piniella

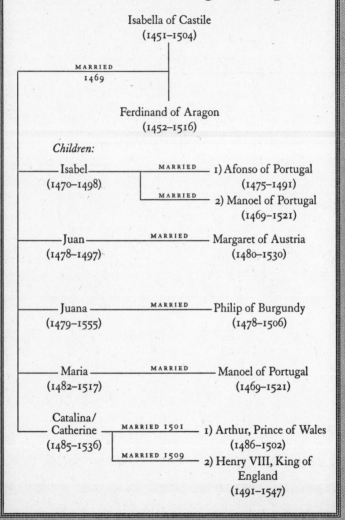

The Catholic Kings of Spain

Isabella of Castile
(1451–1504)

MARRIED
1469

Ferdinand of Aragon
(1452–1516)

Children:

Isabel ————— MARRIED — 1) Afonso of Portugal
(1470–1498)   (1475–1491)
                        MARRIED — 2) Manoel of Portugal
                                    (1469–1521)

Juan ————— MARRIED — Margaret of Austria
(1478–1497)   (1480–1530)

Juana ————— MARRIED — Philip of Burgundy
(1479–1555)   (1478–1506)

Maria ————— MARRIED — Manoel of Portugal
(1482–1517)   (1469–1521)

Catalina/
Catherine ——— MARRIED 1501 — 1) Arthur, Prince of Wales
(1485–1536)   (1486–1502)
                        MARRIED 1509 — 2) Henry VIII, King of
                                    England
                                    (1491–1547)

The Tudors

OF ENGLAND

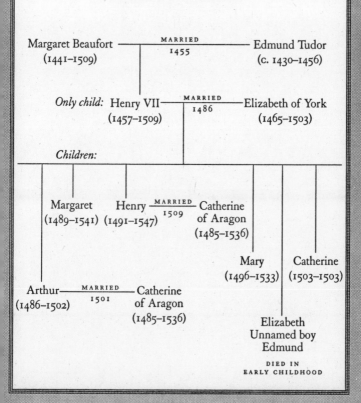

Margaret Beaufort ——— MARRIED 1455 ——— Edmund Tudor
(1441–1509)   (c. 1430–1456)

Only child: Henry VII ——— MARRIED 1486 ——— Elizabeth of York
(1457–1509)   (1465–1503)

Children:

Margaret   Henry ——— MARRIED 1509 ——— Catherine
(1489–1541)   (1491–1547)   of Aragon
                                                          (1485–1536)

                                                                    Mary   Catherine
                                                              (1496–1533)   (1503–1503)

Arthur ——— MARRIED 1501 ——— Catherine
(1486–1502)   of Aragon
                                                  (1485–1536)

                                                              Elizabeth
                                                          Unnamed boy
                                                              Edmund

                                                          DIED IN
                                                  EARLY CHILDHOOD

PROLOGUE

Buckden Towers, Huntingdonshire, England
December 1533

Betrayal. Cruelty. Loss.

These words echo in the dark chambers of my heart, echo again through the halls of this moldering castle where my husband, the king, has made me a prisoner. How could he turn against me like this? The man I loved—and love still—has forbidden me to see our daughter, Mary, forbidden me even to write to her or receive any messages from her. He has ordered most of my servants dismissed and sent away all but a handful of my loyal ladies-in-waiting. He has denied me all visitors save those he sends. Today he has sent Charles Brandon, duke of Suffolk.

Beyond this oaken door Brandon waits with orders from the king to exact an oath from my few remaining servants to address me as "the Princess Dowager." No longer may they call me Queen Catherine. Those who refuse are to be dismissed.

In this manner the king thinks he will break my will.

After more than twenty years of marriage, King Henry VIII demanded my agreement that our union was not and had never been valid, that I was not and had never been his true and legitimate wife, and that our daughter is, therefore, a bastard. This, so that he could divorce me and marry the witch, Anne Boleyn, and make her his queen. This, so that his new "wife" could provide him with a son and legitimate heir to the throne.

I am an aging woman, my forty-eight years weighing heavily upon me. But well I remember when my husband and I first met: he a mere boy of ten years, I six years older but still only a girl myself. I was young and eager, full of hope for the future. As it turned out, he *was* my future.

In the first years of our marriage, King Henry jousted with my sleeve on his lance and called himself "Sir Loyal Heart," proclaiming to all the world his love for me. As the years passed, I became his closest confidante, his most trusted adviser. My love for him grew, even when his affections strayed to other women. Although it wounded me deeply to know that one of them had borne him the son he so devoutly desired, I survived those wounds, for I was his wife. *I was his queen.*

Now, after twenty-four years, all he wants from me

is my compliance, my assent to release him from his marriage vows. He would have me remove myself to a convent and live out the rest of my days in prayer and contemplation. He would have me deny that I am the queen.

Anne, the woman he now calls "wife" and "queen," has borne him a daughter these three months past. They have named her Elizabeth. I can imagine his bitter disappointment. I can even imagine her despair, her apologies, her promises.

On the other side of the door to this chamber, Brandon, Henry's oldest friend, first pleads, then threatens.

"Tell my husband, the king, that I will not yield!" I call to him.

Brandon shouts, "If you do not yield, then I have orders to escort you to Somersham."

Somersham! A manor house even more remote and wretched than this dour place, surrounded by a stinking moat into which the garderobe empties.

"If you wish to take me, my lord of Suffolk, you will have to break down this door."

"You are the most obdurate of women!"

Silence ensues. From the latticed window of my chamber, I can look down upon the wild and desolate Fens where men have gathered from surrounding farms and villages, carrying scythes and pitchforks. They wait warily. They will not allow me to be harmed. My people love me, if my king does not.

It is deathly quiet. Perhaps the duke and his men have gone; likely they will return. I gather my memories. Our stories, Henry's and mine, are as intricately woven together as our lives—stories of love and loyalty, of betrayal and cruelty, and always, always, of loss. These are the stories I remember.

CHAPTER 1

Voyage to England

Richmond Palace, July 1501

Henry, duke of York, raised his heavy longbow and squinted at the target. There was a sharp twang as he released the bowstring, a sweet whistle of the flying arrow, a mellow thunk as it struck just outside the center circle. Henry smiled. His brother Arthur, prince of Wales, grimaced. Henry, a week past his tenth birthday, already stood taller and stronger than Arthur, who was five years older. Henry was a better shot, too. This clearly annoyed his brother, as Henry hoped it would.

"What of Princess Catherine?" asked Henry, while Brandon took his shot, a deliberately middling one. "She is coming, is she not?"

"I do not know, York," Arthur replied glumly. "She was promised before you were even born. She was supposed to marry me when I turned fourteen, and that was nearly a year ago. In her last letter she wrote that she would leave Granada in May. That was months ago, and as you can see, she is still not here." Arthur's shot was poor, worse than Brandon's.

Henry nocked another arrow. "She writes to you, then?" This time his aim was careless and the arrow hit wide of the mark, causing Arthur to smile. The smile faded when Brandon's next shot struck near Henry's first.

"Of course she writes to me. Her Latin is impeccable, and her handwriting is the most elegant imaginable." Arthur's next shot flew truer than the last, but no better than Henry's.

"Perhaps the letters are dictated by her tutors." Henry could not resist adding, "As are yours."

Arthur threw him a hard look. "My Latin is admirable."

"Not so good as mine, though." Henry's third arrow struck precisely in the center of the target; Brandon split Henry's arrow in two.

Arthur ignored Henry's remark, but when his third attempt missed the straw butt entirely, he stalked off toward the palace. Henry and their friend, Brandon, followed.

"Father is sending me back to the Marches tomorrow, did you know that?" said Arthur. "How lucky for you both, to remain here with the family, while I must live in cold and lonely old Ludlow Castle and pretend to exercise some authority over those wild Welshmen!" He slapped his glove against his thigh. "So far from London I might as well be in the Orient."

Henry rarely showed much sympathy for Arthur, who enjoyed their father's favor and all the privileges due a prince. Arthur would one day be king of England, while Henry would never be more than a duke—a fact that often bothered Henry, who secretly believed he would make a much better king than Arthur. For a moment, though, he felt a tug of brotherly compassion.

"Soon Princess Catherine will come," he said, laying his hand on Arthur's thin shoulder, "and then surely you will be less lonely, and Ludlow will be endurable."

On the morning of the seventeenth of August, *anno Domini* 1501, I stood on the windswept deck, biting my lip to keep it from trembling. I stared at the shore to etch on my memory this last glimpse of my country. Tears blurred my eyes and threatened to spill over. Six full-rigged ships prepared to sail from La Coruña, the westernmost port city of Spain, carrying me and my entourage toward England.

The anchors rattled on their heavy chains, the sails snapped like gunshots as strong gusts filled them, and the tall masts creaked and groaned. Minstrels pranced about the deck, playing their guitars and flutes and tabors. Sailors shouted as they cast off the ropes, the last fragile ties with my homeland. Scores of knights and archers who had accompanied us on the three-month journey across Spain stood stiffly on the shore, growing smaller as the ships headed out to sea. Directly north lay my future as the wife of Arthur, prince of Wales.

The admiral himself had escorted me and my duenna, Doña Elvira Manuel, to the royal cabin that had been outfitted with every luxury. Before he left us, he assured us that we would be both safe and comfortable there.

"But, my lady princess," he had said, scanning skies that were milky blue but cloudless, "I can offer you no assurance of the weather. The Bay of Biscay is well known for its thunderous waves and turbulent seas and unpredictable winds."

For three days the winds held steady, and our little fleet skimmed over the calm surface of the water, the motion gentle and soothing. I strolled the deck, conversing with my favorite maids of honor—Inez de Venegas, the most intelligent; Maria de Salinas, the bravest and most loyal; and Francesca de Caceres, the gayest, most high-spirited. Doña Elvira watched over us—but especially me—with the eyes of a hawk and the ears of a hare.

"I feel homesick already," Inez confessed. "Do you not also, my lady Catalina?"

I gazed straight ahead and lifted my chin, attempting to appear braver than I felt. "I cannot allow myself to be homesick," I said. "One day all of you will return to Spain to marry, but I shall live in England for the rest of my life."

"Oh, no!" cried Maria. "I promise I will never leave you!"

"Maybe an English duke will ask for your hand, Maria," said Francesca. "You will marry well and become a duchess."

"Not a duke—that would be too far above you," Inez pointed out. "But a baron would be nice."

"We shall all marry English barons," Francesca declared. "And stay in England with our lady princess."

"I hear the weather is dreadful," sighed Maria, a small girl with delicate features.

"Cold and rainy," agreed Inez, who was tall and awkward. "And you must not drink the water. I am told the English drink ale morning, noon, and night. It is said to be very bitter."

For a time we stared glumly at the sea. The wind had shifted, stirring up lacy whitecaps on the dark water.

"Let us speak of something cheerful," Francesca suggested. "My lady Catalina, tell us what you know of your intended husband."

"Nothing," I said, attempting to laugh. "Padre Alessandro tells me that, when he visited England as a youth, he found the king tall and manly with blond hair and the queen fair and well favored. From that evidence my chaplain concludes that Prince Arthur must surely have inherited his parents' noble bearing and fine features."

"And his letters?" asked Maria. "What have you learned from them?"

I thought of the letters I carried in a fine leather case trimmed in silver. The letters declared Prince Arthur's ardent love for me in Latin as stiffly formal as though he were writing to a foreign ambassador. "He calls me his wife and says he is impatient for my arrival," I said.

"Love letters?" teased Francesca boldly.

But Doña Elvira's long beak of a nose had already

begun to twitch at the scent of impropriety, and we turned our conversation to other matters.

On the fourth day at sea the sky darkened to a bruised purple, erratic winds tore at the sails, and the waters that had seemed so pleasant only hours earlier turned violently angry.

As the wooden ship plunged from the crest of one monstrous wave to the trough of the next, I huddled in my cabin with my ladies and Doña Elvira. Terrified, we clung to our pallets, watching helplessly as our belongings were flung about and seawater surged past the bulkhead.

I clutched at my mattress, weak with seasickness and terror, listening to Doña Elvira and Maria reciting their prayers, Francesca weeping, and Inez calling for her mother.

The sounds outside our cabin were terrible. I heard the shouts of the sailors and the dreadful cry, "Man overboard!" I heard an awful boom, like the firing of a cannon—later I learned that it was a topmast breaking off and dragging ropes and sails into the sea. I despaired of the fate of the other ships. How could any of us survive such a dreadful battering?

The storm raged for three days, perhaps longer—I had lost count. Hourly I expected to die and cried out for God's mercy. Hourly I was grateful to find myself still alive. Then suddenly the skies cleared and the troubled sea was tranquil again. Miraculously, we had survived.

The admiral appeared at the door of the royal cabin, his eyes exhausted and his face haggard and bloody. His left arm dangled uselessly. He looked us over hastily, and assured that we were all alive and uninjured, told us that the fleet must return to port as quickly as possible. The seams were opening, the ship was taking on water, the sails hung in tatters. Worse yet—and here his voice broke—one of the ships was unaccounted for.

We looked at each other, stricken. Which ship? Whom had we lost?

Doña Elvira, whose usual response was complaint and blame, insisted that we had been poorly cared for; she would see the responsible party punished. I opened my mouth to protest such a harsh view and then thought better of it—I had learned in the past weeks that disagreeing with Doña Elvira often made matters worse. "Let us fall to our knees and thank God that we have survived," I said. "And when we set foot again on dry land, we shall thank God—and our brave seamen—for that, too."

The next day the five ships limped into Laredo, Spain's largest northern port, and we straggled ashore. To our relief, the missing ship appeared only hours after the others, though a number of her men had been lost at sea. The company of grateful survivors—including the sixty persons who would stay with me to become the

permanent members of my household in England together with all the others who would return to Spain
after the wedding—gathered on the beach to hear a
mass of thanksgiving said by the archbishop.

While workmen labored to repair the damaged
ships, caulk the leaking seams with tar, and replace the
missing masts and rigging, seamen unloaded thirty
leather-bound wooden chests with my initials ham-
mered on the lids in brass nails. I knew what was in
those trunks. Some were filled with my gowns and jewels, while others contained flagons and ewers, platters
and goblets, candlesticks and candelabra, all wrought of
silver or gold, representing a portion of my dowry. Di-
vided among the chests were two hundred kidskin
bags, each containing five hundred gold escudos—half
of my dowry—to be paid over to King Henry VII on
my wedding day. The balance was to be paid within a
year, part from the plate and jewels, part in escudos to be
sent by my father.

Under the direction of Doña Elvira's husband, Don
Pedro Manrique, every item was unpacked, tallied,
dried, mended, and replaced in new trunks. Meanwhile, we waited.

Weeks passed. My ladies grew dull and restless,
especially Francesca, always the most vigorous and ad-
venturous of them all. When it was discovered that
Francesca had made the acquaintance of one of the
ship's officers and had been seen in conversation with

him, the wrath of Doña Elvira came down upon her. "Are you without shame, Lady Francesca?" she cried. "I am of a mind to send you back to your parents! Let your father deal with you!"

From that time forward, Doña Elvira was relentless in her discipline of Francesca. And Francesca was frank about her feelings for Doña Elvira. "I neither like nor trust her," Francesca whispered to me. "Anyone so suspicious of others is unlikely to be trustworthy herself."

"I am certain our duenna intends it for our own good," I replied, though in my heart I agreed with Francesca.

For a full month, while the ships made ready once more, I waited restlessly to resume the voyage to my new life as the bride of Arthur, prince of Wales, and the future queen of England.

At the end of September, several days before we set sail for the second time, Captain Stephen Brett of the English navy arrived at Laredo, dispatched by King Henry VII to search for his son's missing bride. Captain Brett would guide us across the Bay of Biscay, grown even more dangerous now with autumn storms rolling in from the Atlantic Ocean, to safety in England.

"You have nothing further to fear, mistress," the grizzled captain assured me, displaying a smile of blackened teeth. "You will shortly be on English soil, and all will be well."

"I pray that you are right, sir," I replied through an interpreter, though I had no confidence that he was.

As it turned out, the captain was wrong. On the last day of the voyage, the seas again turned treacherous. The six ships were lashed by one furious squall after another as thunder boomed and lightning crackled ominously close by.

"Surely this is an ill omen, my lady," gasped Francesca, dark eyes wide with fright. "Perhaps God does not want you to go to England after all."

"Perhaps He is testing me," I replied, struggling not to let my fear overwhelm me. "And I shall not be found wanting."

The storms ceased as suddenly as they had begun, and hours later the Spanish ships entered Plymouth harbor under a bright sun, led by Captain Brett in the pilot boat. Dressed in a gown that had somehow escaped a second soaking, I waited in the waist of the ship with the count of Cabra, the bishop of Majorca, and the archbishop of Santiago, the three who would stand in place of my parents at my marriage ceremony. The ladies of my court, miserable in their damp clothes, arranged themselves behind me according to rank. I had never felt worse in my life—my head throbbed, my stomach churned, my legs were so weak that I could scarcely stand upright. Doña Elvira braced herself to catch me if I should falter.

A huge crowd had gathered on the wharf, watching as the ship was warped in by seamen pulling hard on stout ropes. "I shall never willingly set foot on board a ship as long as I live," I whispered to Maria, whose pallor surely reflected my own.

In the front of the cheering throng, feet wide apart, stood a short, round man arrayed in a red velvet cloak and a hat with a plume nearly as long as his arm. Whoever he was, he swept off the hat as he fell to his knees and shouted up to me. I wanted nothing more than a warm, dry place to lie down, but despite my wretchedness I behaved as my mother had taught me: I smiled and nodded through the official speeches, words that I did not recognize but believed I understood.

Welcome to England!

CHAPTER 2

The Bright Star of Spain

Richmond Palace, October 1501

Several days' journey to the east of Plymouth, Henry slid an ebony bishop across the chessboard. Brandon peered down hard at his few remaining pieces, and Henry congratulated himself that within the next move or two Brandon would fall into his trap. If Henry could not defeat Brandon at archery, he could easily do so at chess. Brandon himself readily conceded that he had no talent for the game.

Brandon had been brought by the king as a companion for Arthur, but even before Arthur was packed off to the Marches, Brandon had begun to spend much of his time with Henry. An orphan lacking both position and title, Brandon was a year older than the prince, six years older than Henry, and a superb athlete. He could outwrestle both of them—Arthur was no challenge—outride them, out-shoot them, win every tennis match. But Henry was confident that in a few years he would likely best Brandon at every sport.

The duke loved Brandon like a brother—perhaps even more, but he could never admit that, even to himself—and the affection was returned. "My grandfather was once your father's standard-bearer at Bosworth Field," Brandon often told him. "My grandfather died defending your father."

Henry enjoyed hearing that story and understood its significance: His father had not inherited the throne; he had won it on Bosworth Field by killing the usurper, King Richard III. Exactly as I would have done, thought Henry. He could not imagine Arthur fighting to the death for anything, even the throne.

Henry barely glanced up from the board when a messenger clattered through the gallery with a letter for the king. Moments later the king burst out of his chambers and rushed to the queen's chambers, shouting, "She is here! She is here! The princess has arrived at Plymouth, and she is making her way toward London!"

A fresh messenger was dispatched immediately to carry the news to Arthur at Ludlow. Long-laid plans to welcome Princess Catherine to London with all the pomp and ceremony due the daughter of the monarchs of Spain must be set in motion. Arrangements for the wedding must now go forward. The king stomped about, shouting orders and announcing that no expense was to be spared, so great was the *importance of this event. This announcement surprised Henry and Brandon, both aware of how closefisted the king was known to be. Henry felt a sudden, sharp twinge of jealousy—Arthur was getting all the attention, as usual.*

But Henry said nothing and concentrated again on the chessboard, where Brandon had finally made his move.

"Check," said Henry.

MY JOURNEY HAD BEGUN IN MAY OF 1501 WHEN I left Granada. At the farewell celebration, bright flowers decorated every corner of the Alhambra, the great square-towered Moorish citadel at the foot of the looming Sierra Nevada. Every morning for a week I awakened to the smell of roasting meat, and every night, after we had feasted on venison and spring lamb and cakes made of pomegranates and almonds, my ladies and I danced for the members of the court. As much as I loved the feasting and dancing, each day was a painful reminder that I would soon set out on a journey to a distant land and might never see my parents again.

My mother, Queen Isabella, had been preparing me for my departure since my betrothal to Prince Arthur at the age of two. I was the last of her children to marry, and she was reluctant to let me go. The wounds inflicted by the deaths of my eldest sister Isabel, of Prince Juan, my only brother, and most recently of Isabel's little son were still fresh in my mother's heart. My sister Maria had left for Portugal seven months earlier to marry Isabel's widower, King Manoel, and my next eldest sister, Juana, had been in the Netherlands for almost five years as wife of Philip of Burgundy. Once I passed my fifteenth birthday, my mother could no longer postpone the inevitable. When the moment came for me to take my leave, she was unable to hold back her tears. I could scarcely bear to see the pain written so clearly on her dear face.

"You will be in good hands," my mother assured me, as she assured herself, and named some of those familiar faces who would accompany me: Padre Alessandro, who had been my lifelong tutor and chaplain, Juan de Cuero as household treasurer, and so on. "I can think of no lady better to serve as your duenna than Doña Elvira. She has been a member of my court for many years, and I know her character to be above reproach. We are little acquainted with the English and their ways, and I trust Doña Elvira to protect your reputation resolutely."

I bowed my head. I did not like Doña Elvira. She was harsh and tyrannical. But I would not go against my mother's will. I said nothing, keeping my head lowered so that she would not notice my distress. "We shall write one another often, shall we not?" I murmured, trying unsuccessfully not to weep.

"Of course we shall send letters, dear Catalina, and I shall always be happy to hear news of your life. I have great faith that the training I have given you and the advisers I am sending with you will provide the wisdom and sensibility you will require as wife, mother, and queen. In difficult times bring to mind my words and the sound of my voice. In that way, I shall always be present for you." Then my mother gave me her blessing, kissed my forehead, my eyelids, my lips, and turned away. "Go, Catalina," my mother said in a shaking voice. "Go now, and quickly."

I was weeping so hard I could scarcely find my way from her chamber. But I knew I must dry my tears and calm myself. When I felt able, I knelt before my father, the king, who showed as little feeling as the stones of the ancient citadel. He seldom did, though I believed I knew what was in his heart—I had always been his favorite daughter. I took his hand in both of mine and kissed it. My father merely frowned and made the sign of the cross over me.

Mounted on a mule in a red saddle-chair, I rode for the last time through lush gardens of jasmine and oleander, passed by the groves of almond, lime, and fig, and soon left behind the shade of the tall cypress trees of Andalucía. Now that the anguish of the parting was over, my thoughts turned toward the future. I was excited to be on my way, eager to begin my new life as the future queen of England.

The long procession—noblemen and churchmen, my maids of honor, tutors, chaplain, treasurer, equerry, majordomo, and duenna, plus innumerable knights and archers, countless cooks and bakers, servitors and muleteers, minstrels, and fools—stretched farther than I could see. Day after day, as the procession wound over rugged mountains and plodded across the stark and dusty plains of Castilla, we endured searing heat and sudden downpours. My ladies took turns riding with me in the royal litter, borne by sure-footed mules and curtained with silks to protect us from the dust and the relentless sun. Each night we stopped at convents where I and my attendants were accommodated. Our servants camped in the open fields.

On those nights when sleep would not come, I lay in my bed and practiced a few useful phrases Padre Alessandro had taught me: *Good day, my lord* and *Good evening, my lady, If it please you, sire* and *Thank you, madam.*

"You will learn quickly once you are living among the English," the chaplain assured me. I could only hope that he was right.

"They probably will not call you Catalina," he had said as we prepared for the journey.

"What will they call me then?"

"Catherine is, I believe, the closest the English will come to it. *C-A-T-H-E-R-I-N-E.*"

So I was to lose my name! The same had happened to my sister, Juana, when she married Philip of Burgundy and went to live in the Netherlands. Juana became *Joanna*—not a pretty name, I thought, and so difficult for the Spanish tongue to pronounce.

"Catherine," I whispered in the darkness. No more Catalina. *Catherine.*

Waiting for me in Plymouth and the first to welcome me in my own tongue was Pedro de Ayala, my parents' ambassador to Scotland. I had expected to be met by the ambassador to England, Rodrigo Gonzales de Puebla, who had negotiated my marriage contract and stood in my stead at the betrothal ceremony years ago. But when I inquired about him, the elegantly dressed Ayala merely waved his hand dismissively. "Don Rodrigo will, no doubt, greet you in London," he said, explaining that he, Ayala, had decided to leave Scotland for England. "Life here is so much more pleasant than up north."

Later I learned that each of the two ambassadors harbored a deep dislike for the other, and Ayala had managed to outwit his rival by riding out to Plymouth when he heard that my ships were bound there. Puebla had been left behind in London, unaware of my arrival.

After a few days of rest in Plymouth—to give the royal couriers time to carry the news to the king—my company set out for London.

"It will be a slow journey with numerous stops along the way," explained Ayala, "to allow my lady princess time to regain her strength. Also," he added, "we shall give the English an opportunity to see for themselves the woman who shall one day be their queen."

We rode in a light drizzle to our first stop, a country manor in Exeter where our host had prepared an elaborate feast. With a great flourish the lord of the manor presented me with a silver goblet filled to the brim with a golden liquid that smelled unpleasantly sour. He proposed a toast.

"Their finest English ale," Ayala murmured close to my ear.

I raised the goblet to my lips and tried to drink. The bitterness brought tears to my eyes. "This must be what was offered on the sponge to our Lord on the cross," I whispered to Ayala. As good manners required, I drained the goblet to the last drop to the cheers of those around me.

After a fortnight in Exeter we continued our journey eastward. We rode on mules brought from Spain; I seated in my red saddle-chair. Doña Elvira insisted that my face remain veiled, as befitted a royal maiden. A number of English ladies rode with us on horseback, dressed in bright velvets, their faces bared to anyone who cared to look. Here I discovered another odd custom: English ladies mounted their sidesaddles from the left while Spanish ladies mounted from the right. They sat on opposite sides of their horses and often rode facing away from one another.

How different it all was from Spain! The great procession moved past dark, forbidding forests and open fields, past green pastures crowded with grazing sheep and cows, past the thatched cottages of the country folk. The roads were no more than rough paths worn by sheep and cows, and the mud was already deep on my mule's withers. The ever present mist clung to my skin like wet silk, and at the end of each day's travel my gown was sodden.

I struggled to wrap my tongue around the strange names of the towns and villages through which we passed: Crewkerne, Sherborne, Shaftesbury. Such tumult greeted me! Cheering crowds surged around us, bells rang clamorously, men tossed their caps into the air, and women held aloft their little ones to give the children a glimpse of me.

From the center of each village rose a church steeple, and close by stood the sumptuous manor houses of noblemen who welcomed us graciously and served us banquets and more ale.

At each stop additional knights joined the procession. Commoners, too, often accompanied us, walking from one village to the next and then returning home to their labors. I found them a boisterous lot, the women as noisy as their husbands, and saw that they could be easily roused to brawling among themselves. Still, I sensed their goodwill.

As we made our way toward London, I thought constantly about Prince Arthur and wondered anxiously what he would think of me. The more I saw of English ladies in their bright colors and unveiled faces, the more I worried that my future husband would not find me to his liking. I was not tall, but I was well formed with a long, graceful neck and a narrow waist; the journey had been so arduous that I was no longer so plump as when I left Granada. I had my mother's wide gray eyes, bright smile, and pale, unblemished skin. The English ladies covered their hair with headdresses, but Spanish ladies took pride in their tresses. Bright as copper, lustrous as silk, falling nearly to my waist, my hair was my glory.

Each night I prayed earnestly for wisdom and patience and humility. I prayed that I would be a dutiful wife to Arthur, an obedient daughter to the king and queen, and an agreeable sister to the prince's younger brother and sisters. After I had prayed for the health and well-being of my family in Spain and for all of those who traveled with me, I allowed myself to make one small, personal request: I prayed that Arthur would find me appealing. I dreaded looking into his eyes and finding disappointment rather than delight as he lifted my wedding veil and gazed at my face for the first time.

I thought again of the letters Prince Arthur had written me during our long betrothal. In the small hours of the night before we were to arrive in Dogmersfield, our last stop before London, I crept from my bed—taking care not to waken Doña Elvira, who snored nearby—and opened the leather and silver case in which I kept Arthur's letters. Unfolding the last one I had received, I held the parchment close to a candle flame and read his words again: *Let your coming to me be hastened that instead of being absent we may be present with each other, and the love conceived between us and the wished-for joys may reap their proper fruit.*

Perhaps they were not his own words, but surely they expressed the true feelings of his heart. Or so I promised myself, before I returned the letter to its case and returned myself to my bed.

CHAPTER 3

Dogmersfield

Richmond Palace, November 1501

Every day a mud-splattered messenger galloped to the palace to inform King Henry of the Spanish princess's progress toward London.

But the king was restless, dissatisfied. He questioned the messengers closely: "What does the princess look like? How does she appear to you? Is she comely? Is she in good health? Is her neck plump, her skin white and unblemished? Her breath sweet?"

The messengers could reply only that they themselves had not seen the princess, who was being kept in strict seclusion by her governess and appeared in public with her face hidden beneath a veil.

After three weeks of impatient waiting, the king announced to his privy council, "I shall go and see the princess for myself."

A messenger was dispatched to Ludlow, informing the prince of Wales that he and his gentlemen were to rendezvous with the king and his council at Dogmersfield, where the Spanish princess was resting. Once they had assembled, they would proceed to the bishop's palace to call upon her and her retinue.

Henry observed all of this, speculating with Brandon what the bride might be like. "I wish that I could have a look at her first, before Arthur does."

"Why?" asked Brandon. "You are not the one who is marrying her."

"Because I am curious," Henry had explained, adding with a wicked grin, "and because it always upsets Arthur when I am ahead of him at anything."

When he believed the time was right, Henry appealed to his father. "And I, Father my lord? Am I to accompany you?"

The king replied gruffly, "No, York. You shall stay here with your mother and sisters and prepare to greet the princess when she arrives in London."

"Yes, my lord." Henry managed to hide his anger and disappointment and bowed deeply, kneeling three times as he backed out of his father's privy chamber.

In a foul mood, he went in search of Brandon and found him waiting for him in the courtyard. "I have in mind a game of tennis," Henry said. "Perhaps today I shall show myself to be the better player."

"Perhaps, my lord," said Brandon, smiling.

Still angry at his father for not taking him to Dogmersfield, Henry smashed shots wildly in all directions and threw down his racquet in a temper. He hated to lose, even to Brandon, but he was not jealous of Brandon, as he was of Arthur. Brandon did not even have a title, so what was there to envy?

NEARLY A MONTH AFTER I STEPPED ASHORE AT PLYMouth, my rain-soaked entourage reached the village of Dogmersfield. For the past several days I had abandoned my mule for the shelter of my litter.

The archbishop of Bath had invited us to lodge at his palace. I was no sooner settled into the royal apartments, my ladies drying out in their chambers, and Doña Elvira quartered within hearing of my every word and movement, than the king's messenger arrived. I broke the royal seal and swiftly read the letter: King Henry was at that very hour on his way to the bishop's palace, accompanied by his privy council and his son, the prince of Wales! I read the message a second time, scarcely believing the words. Surely, I must have time to make myself ready! I passed the letter to Doña Elvira even before she could insist upon it and began to think how I might best prepare for the meeting.

I felt happily excited, but my duenna was aghast. "Absolutely not!" she exclaimed. "Has the king taken leave of his senses? It is the custom of our people that neither the bridegroom nor his father may lay eyes upon the bride until the archbishop pronounces the benediction at the end of the marriage ceremony! I gave my solemn word to your parents that you would be treated with the respect due the daughter of the kings of Spain. King Henry shall not see you, nor shall Prince Arthur."

Before I could reply, Doña Elvira summoned the ambassador. Ayala entered my chambers looking drowsy, as though his sleep had been interrupted. When the duenna thrust the king's letter into his hands, Ayala merely yawned, shrugged, and returned the letter to me with a lazy smile.

"Doña Elvira, what seems to you an outrage is, to our friend the king of England, an entirely justifiable request. The English set great store by the beauty of women, and King Henry no doubt wishes to assure himself that the mother of future kings of the realm is not only strong and healthy but comely as well."

"That is an outrage!" Furiously, Doña Elvira stamped her foot. "An insult to our lady princess!" Once Doña Elvira began her tirade, complaining in her strident voice about the abominable manners of the barbarous English, there was no stopping her. I paced distractedly, not knowing what to do. The two were still arguing when a page announced that King Henry and his retinue were entering the gates of Dogmersfield.

The duenna's usually pale face flushed bright red and then turned deathly white, as though she might faint. Thinking of my mother and her unwavering calm in difficult situations, I summoned my courage and instructed Ayala to delay the king as long as possible.

"Tell the king that the princess is resting and can see no one. From what you say, he will no doubt insist. You must protest, the king will press harder, and by then I shall be ready." Doña Elvira, who had collapsed onto a bench, seemed unable to object.

Quickly I called for my maidservants to dress me. From the courtyard came the clatter of horses' hoofs and the blare of trumpets announcing the king's arrival. Doña Elvira recovered herself and watched, shocked into silence but glowering her disapproval, as my women hastily laced up my red satin gown overlaid with black lace. Inez brushed my hair until it gleamed, and Maria de Salinas clasped a necklace of rubies and diamonds about my neck.

I stole quietly to the oaken doors leading into the Great Hall of the palace and listened through the crack as the ambassador delivered the message to the king. The king replied in words I could not understand, though his commanding tone was clear enough. Ayala repeated loudly in our language, "Tell the lady's governess that the king of England will see the princess, even if she is in her bed."

He is a bully, I thought, and my courage nearly failed me. I heard Doña Elvira suck in her breath. My ladies, eyes round with excitement, draped a veil of finest gossamer silk over my head and face. My legs trembling, and showing more confidence than I felt, I signaled for the doors to be opened. As the guards swung them back, I paused to give the king an opportunity to look at me before I slowly lifted the veil to reveal my face. I was at once engaged by King Henry's intense blue-gray eyes, eyes that showed intelligence, shrewdness, and perhaps a streak of cruelty. For a moment I stared into those arresting eyes. Then, I threw back my veil entirely and smiled.

The king, regal even in robes that were caked with mud, returned my smile. I curtsied deeply. The king bowed low and kissed my hand. We greeted one another, I in Spanish and the king in English, and though neither of us understood the words of the other, we understood the meaning: He found me pleasing, and I found him pleased.

But where was the prince? It was Arthur I most wished to see! My eyes searched the crowded hall for some sign. Then, even as I wished it, trumpets proclaimed the arrival of the prince of Wales. My heart began to pound as the doors opened and into the Great Hall walked a pretty blond boy, a slender youth with delicate features.

I hesitated. *Who—?*

The boy smiled and stepped forward. Arthur!

He is little more than a child, I thought, struggling to conceal my surprise; *a beautiful boy.* Nearer he came, his face alight with pleasure. The vast hall had fallen silent, as though every breath were drawn and held. The prince knelt before me on one knee. I bent my trembling knees in a curtsy. The boy reached for my hand and raised it to his lips. Our eyes met. I returned his smile. The assembled company, English and Spanish, broke into cheers.

Both the prince and his father made formal speeches in English, which were repeated in Latin by one of the English bishops. I could have easily replied in Latin, but it would have been unseemly for me to show myself more eloquent than the king. And so I delivered my responses in Spanish and allowed the Spanish bishops to turn them into Latin phrases more pompous and ornate than any I would have thought to utter.

As my future husband and I stood side by side during the speeches of welcome, our hands barely touching, I realized Arthur had to look *up* at me—I was nearly half a head taller. When it was our turn to speak to one another, Prince Arthur made a little speech, welcoming me as his most beloved wife. I grasped only a little of what he said, for though the Latin words poured easily from his lips, his manner of speech sounded strange to my ears. And his voice! It was the voice of a boy who had not yet become a man. Still, I smiled as though these were the most delightful words that had ever fallen upon my ears. And when I replied, I could read the look of perplexity on his face: My Latin words were as strange to him as his were to me.

The speeches were done at last. I invited the English company to join me and my people at a reception, after they had had a chance to refresh themselves and to change their wet and muddy garments.

As soon as they had gone, I began to give orders for the reception. We would have a supper, I decided, less sumptuous than a banquet, as there was no time to prepare for that. Then I would call upon my minstrels to play, and we would have dancing.

Doña Elvira continued to frown, cluck her tongue, and mutter darkly, "Highly improper! Their majesties, the kings of Spain, would certainly not approve."

But I believed that my mother most certainly *would* approve—*When in doubt, behave like a queen, with authority!* she had taught me—and my plans were set in motion.

As the palace bustled with activity, I turned to Maria and Inez and Francesca, who fluttered around me, their excitement barely contained. "Tell me, please," I begged them, "which gown I should wear this evening to show me off to best advantage to the young man I shall soon marry!"

They offered their opinions—each different—but I could see they were more concerned about what they themselves should wear for this first introduction to the young Englishmen.

At last I settled upon a gown of tawny velvet bordered in black and silver, the sleeves lined in pale yellow silk. Doña Elvira insisted that I must again wear a veil. I protested that English women did not practice this custom, and perhaps I should begin to conform to their foreign ways.

"Absolutely not!" my duenna cried, her voice harsh as a crow's. "You will disgrace yourself and the good name of your most honorable parents!" To mollify her, I chose a mantilla of sheerest black lace. Besides, a mantilla always made a woman more beautiful.

I longed to sit beside the prince, to converse quietly with him without dozens listening, to puzzle out together the meaning of his words, to learn more about this pretty young boy. But that was out of the question. Custom required me to sit with Doña Elvira and my ladies at one end of the hall and the king, the prince, and their gentlemen at the opposite end.

When the remains of the meal had been cleared away, I clapped my hands to summon our minstrels. Playing upon flutes, *vihuelas,* and other stringed instruments, the musicians began a stately *zarabanda*. My ladies and I took our places and began the dance, my feet moving deftly through steps I had rehearsed since childhood. I hoped that my skill and grace would make a favorable impression upon Arthur and his father, whose faces remained hidden in shadow.

Then King Henry called upon his musicians. Prince Arthur led out one of the English ladies, a portly woman, heavily powdered and rouged. He danced well, I thought, but I could see that their stately dances varied greatly from ours. One day soon, I promised myself, I would master these English dances, and the language, too. But for the moment I was content.

The evening passed more swiftly than I could have

imagined, alternating between Spanish and English music and dance, both growing more and more lively as the hours sped by. Without looking in the direction of Doña Elvira—I knew well what her expression would be—I threw back my veil as we began one of our most energetic dances. When we had finished and returned breathless to our seats, Inez leaned close and whispered, "He cannot help but adore you, my lady princess. You are as flushed and lovely as a summer rose!"

Long after midnight, when the torches were smoking and the candles had burned low on their prickets, we called an end to the entertainments and withdrew to our chambers.

But I was far too excited to sleep. I desired nothing so much as to talk about Arthur, and I refused to give my ladies permission to retire to their beds until they had rendered their opinions: What did they think of the prince? Did they find him handsome? Could they see kindliness in his face?

"His blond curls," Inez said thoughtfully. "I think them his best feature."

"His blue eyes are merry!" offered Maria. "And yes, Catalina, I believe I saw kindliness in them."

"Intelligence and good humor," Francesca added.

"But do you not agree that he appears to be— perhaps of a delicate constitution?" I ventured. "He looks so young, yet I am less than a year older. He reminds me of Prince Juan."

We were all quiet for a moment, remembering my dead brother. Inez had opened her mouth to reply when Doña Elvira swooped down upon us, black eyes glinting fiercely. "Such idle gossip is unworthy of ladies of good breeding," she scolded. "Better that you were at your prayers."

My ladies bowed their heads, but when I glanced toward Francesca, I saw that she had her lips pursed tight, as though she were tasting a lemon fresh from the tree. I was forced to turn away lest I laugh and cause the duenna even greater anger.

After my ladies had retired, I lay in my bed, waiting for sleep and thinking of the events of the day. I remembered my mother's oft repeated story of her first meeting with my father. Disguised as a mule driver, he had ridden from his kingdom in Aragon to marry the princess of Castilla—in defiance of her brother, King Enrique. When Prince Ferdinand arrived at the castle where she awaited him in secret, it was long past midnight. She wore a gown of lavender silk and a ruby necklace and stood bathed in the glow of dozens of candles. As the prince entered her chambers, she exclaimed, "It is he! And all that I could wish!"

When I closed my eyes, Prince Arthur's face appeared, pale and shining, nearly ethereal. *It is the face of an angel,* I thought, drifting off to sleep. *Not a child— an angel! And all that I could wish.*

The next day our goods were again loaded into carts or heaped on the backs of mules. The pelting rain slackened and stopped at last. A little thin sunshine leaked through the fleecy blanket of clouds as I climbed into my litter for the final stage of my journey toward London.

CHAPTER 4

The Princess Bride

Richmond Palace, November 1501

King Henry returned from Dogmersfield in a state of elation. *"I have met the Spanish princess, and I am well satisfied,"* the king informed his wife and daughters, his mother, and his younger son.

"What does she look like?" Princess Margaret wanted to know, but the king merely frowned at her and turned his attention to the duke.

"York," he said, *"I have decided that you shall be the princess's official escort throughout all of the ceremonies. You shall greet her at Kingston-upon-Thames and ride with her into London for the welcoming ceremonies. And you shall be at her side from that time on. You are capable of that, I trust?"*

"I am, my lord," Henry replied, delighted to have been given a major role. He enjoyed these elaborate ceremonies, and he loved being the center of attention—not like Arthur, who seemed to shrink from it. Henry would put on his best performance in honor of the Spanish princess.

"Buckingham will accompany you. He will make sure you get things right."

As though I need Buckingham's help, Henry thought, annoyed that his father felt he needed instruction. But the duke merely bowed to his father and said nothing.

My ENTOURAGE, A BEHEMOTH SWELLING IN SIZE WITH every passing hour, crawled slowly toward Kingston-upon-Thames. The ambassador rode beside me, mounted on a fine gray gelding, keeping me informed of what I should expect.

"King Henry is set to make a splendid show of this," Ayala said, stroking his perfumed beard. "And for a monarch as penurious as he, such extravagance must be painful! This English king does not ever spend a farthing unnecessarily. He is fond of keeping the gold in his own coffers—even fonder than your esteemed father, my lady! But since you are to be the wife of a king and the mother of the future kings of the realm, King Henry has determined that this shall be a sumptuous affair, unequalled in splendor. He is said to be sparing no expense."

Naturally I was curious about plans for the wedding, but when Ayala offered no details beyond "costly," I let my thoughts stray while his sonorous voice glided over me. Occasionally, I caught glimpses of the River Thames, where small boats darted back and forth between north bank and south and larger boats moved with the tide. Flotillas of snowy white swans drifted majestically beneath gray clouds heavy with rain. I missed the sparkling azure of Spanish skies and wondered if there would ever be a time when English skies would be so intensely blue as those in Granada.

Crowds lined the roads, straining for a glimpse of the great procession. Everyone, from humble peasant to most richly accoutered noble, gazed at me with open curiosity. Before I left Spain, my mother had ordered for me a fine wardrobe: elegant gowns made of satins and silks and trimmed with lace and elaborate embroidery; richly furred robes; and costly gems set in ornate necklaces, bracelets, and coronets.

"You must show the people that you are their future queen," my mother had advised me. "I might sleep in a tent and eat humble rations like the soldiers in the field, but I always appear before my people dressed as a *queen*."

As we neared Kingston-upon-Thames, two young pages—one in black and red livery, one in green and white—approached my litter and announced the arrival of the dukes of Buckingham and York. I looked anxiously to Ayala for an explanation. "Green and white are the Tudor colors. Henry, duke of York, is the prince's younger brother. Edward Stafford, duke of Buckingham, is the highest ranking nobleman of England and the king's chamberlain. I believe they have been instructed to escort you into the city."

I sighed, knowing that the leisurely journey from Plymouth was at an end. Throughout the coming weeks, my days would be filled from morning until night with ceremony. I hoped that I would have the strength to endure it.

The procession ground slowly to a standstill, and I climbed down from my litter. I had dressed for this occasion in the pale blue gown and darker blue robe that my duenna had selected. Now she tied a large red hat with lace of gold over my hair, which streamed long and loose down my back. Two black plumes fluttered from the hat. I had observed that none of the English ladies wore hats, and this troubled me. Again I feared that I would appear strange.

My ladies reassured me. "You are every inch a queen," Maria said. "And a beauty," added Francesca, nodding.

Mounting a handsome mule of gleaming black, I rode slowly to the head of my vast procession, which by then numbered several hundred. Approaching from the opposite direction were two richly dressed noblemen, accompanied by their gentlemen-at-arms. Their combined retinues were as large as mine. Ayala, riding by my side, told me what I might expect.

"The king and Prince Arthur are traveling by royal barge from Richmond to Bayard's Castle, where you shall meet the rest of the royal family after the wedding ceremony." The ambassador counted them off on his plump, jeweled fingers: "You have already made the king's acquaintance. His queen, Elizabeth of York, is called Elizabeth the Good by her adoring subjects. The king's mother, Margaret Beaufort, countess of Richmond and Derby, rules the family with an iron fist. I pity the queen, having to put up with such a mother-in-law. I expect you will find a companion, for a short time at least, with Arthur's sister, Margaret, said by all to be her father's favorite. She is just eleven, but he intends to marry her off as soon as possible to James of Scotland. What a lot of barbarians she will find up north! The queen has lost three children in infancy. The youngest surviving is Mary, a child of six."

As the English and Spanish retinues came face-to-face, Ayala broke off his recital to exclaim, "And now, Princess Catalina, you shall meet the duke of York. Just ten years old, and look at him!"

The young duke halted his mount and leaped from the saddle. He bowed low and stood grinning up at me. He was a strapping lad with red-gold hair and merry blue eyes, robustly handsome if not so delicately beautiful as his brother. He spoke to me in a language I recognized as French. Ayala, speaking softly, translated: "The duke of York puts himself at your service, my lady."

"Tell him that the princess of Aragon thanks him."

And so it went, exchanging all the usual polite phrases. After the presentation of the duke of Buckingham and other formalities, the combined procession, numbering perhaps a thousand persons, started off again and advanced with solemn dignity into the great city of London, a city like none I had ever seen.

The narrow, winding streets were badly paved and muddy. I held my breath, both from the overwhelming stench that assaulted me and from the fear that my mule might stumble and toss me into the muck. At every street crossing the procession halted so that I could hear an oration or listen to a choir or witness a spectacle. Knights and squires rode through the crowd, driving back the curious onlookers who pressed ever closer, peering up at me, reaching out to touch me, cheering and shouting incomprehensibly. Though I could make nothing of their words, I sensed their goodwill and waved to them, first with my right hand until it tired and then with my left. Even when both arms ached, I kept on waving.

The next few days passed in a wearying blur of pageants, banquets, and tournaments with Arthur and the English nobility seated at one end of the Great Hall and my people at the other, maintaining the strict separation that formal custom required until after the wedding ceremony. My escort at these events was Henry, duke of York. I knew that he was several years younger than Arthur, but my altogether delightful companion was taller than either of us, by at least a head, and already well muscled. Owing to his size, Henry looked older than Arthur, whom I had not seen since his visit to Dogmersfield, but Henry's demeanor belied his age— he was still a child, an exuberant, high-spirited, ebullient child. I had liked him at once.

As the ceremonies and pageantry droned on, I was sometimes hard put to maintain the discipline that my mother had instilled in me. The life of a queen meant enduring many such occasions. I often wished that I could sit down for a while. I was thirsty but could not ask for something to drink, having deprived myself of liquids for a day so that I would not need to relieve myself. But through it all, the brash young duke of York kept me amused and managed to distract me from my discomfort.

During a pause between a speech by the head of the bakers' guild and the sermon of still another clergyman, Henry said, "Good lady princess, it would make me the happiest boy in all England if you would consent to call me Harry."

"If that is all that is required to make you so happy, dear brother Harry, then I should be happy to oblige," I told him. We spoke in Latin, of course. "But I shall exact a price," I added, suddenly inspired. "You must then call me Catalina." He looked at me quizzically. "My name in Spanish," I explained. I wanted to add "my real name" but did not.

"Catalina," said Henry, trying the name on his tongue. "Catalina."

Henry had an ear for languages that was truly brilliant. He quickly grasped that he and I used the same Latin words but pronounced them differently. He seemed to recognize instinctively what I was saying, and when he replied, he made every effort to speak the words in the same manner I did, so that I could more easily understand him.

"You really should learn to speak French," said Henry. "Everyone at court does. It sounds so much nicer than Latin. Later, of course, you must learn English, too."

"My brother's wife taught me a little French," I admitted. "She said it would be useful to me at the English court. But after he died, my sister-in-law left Spain." I thought of beautiful Margaret of Austria and the gaiety she had brought briefly to our family. "I was fond of her, and if she had stayed, I am sure I would have learned much more from her."

"Then I shall teach you!" Henry promised, and I agreed that I would be happy to learn from him whenever the chance presented itself. "Say *merci,*" instructed the duke. "It means 'thank you.'"

"Merci," I repeated, laughing. "Harry, I believe this is not the time for a French lesson!"

"Why not, my lady Catalina? As good a time as any, I should think. Now say *s'il vous plaît,* meaning 'if it please you.'"

And so we got on merrily, as the duke of York escorted me from one event to another, pointing out things he thought I might find interesting and asking me all manner of questions about my family and life in Spain. I felt that this pleasing youth would become my good friend.

Over and over I wondered what Arthur might be thinking. Was he as curious about me as I was about him? Then I thought of my sisters, all of whom had left home, family, and country to marry. Had they felt as fearful but excited as I felt now on the eve of my wedding? How I wished I could talk with them and confide my tumultuous feelings, on this, my last night as an unmarried woman.

I lay down in the sumptuous bedchamber that had been prepared for me in Bayard's Castle and thought about how my life was about to change. I had already made my confession to Padre Alessandro and finished my prayers, but as I tossed among the silken coverlets, sleepless with an excess of nervous excitement, I prayed again: *Oh, kind and merciful God, if it be your will, let me learn to love Arthur and let him learn to love me!*

Love was not part of the bargain, I knew, but it could happen—it had happened to my sister, Juana, who five years earlier had journeyed to Flanders to marry Philip. I had received a letter from her shortly before I left Granada, confiding that she was so madly in love with her husband that she could scarcely bear for him to leave her sight. Philip's sister, Margaret of Austria, married my brother, Juan. I believed it was a real love match as well. Margaret and I became close friends. But by the summer of 1497, Juan was dead of a fever, and soon after his death, his widow lost the child she carried. Poor Margaret! Before sleep came at last as a blessing, I prayed earnestly that I might be spared such heartache.

Sunday morning began the wedding day I had awaited so long. Cannons boomed to announce my arrival at Saint Paul's Cathedral on this day, the fourteenth of November *anno Domini* 1501. I was dressed in a white satin gown over a farthingale with several hoops made of whalebone that caused the skirt of the gown to stand out from my waist, showing off the intricate gold embroidery and many jewels sewn all over the skirt. My hair and face were covered by a white lace mantilla bordered in gold and pearls. My heart beat almost as loudly as those booming cannons, my stomach churned uneasily, and my shoulders ached from the weight of all that finery. Yet I brimmed with gladness, too. Six months ago I was preparing to leave Granada. Today I would become a wife.

The duke of York, dressed in a suit of white velvet ornamented with gold and jewels, gave me his hand. For a moment we paused at the great west doors of the cathedral. A hush fell over the waiting throngs, and then the trumpeters who had accompanied me from Spain for this occasion blew near-deafening fanfares as we began the long, slow walk down the entire length of the nave. My thoughts leaped once more to my mother, wishing she were here with me to witness this important event, and to my sisters, wondering what they had felt as they made similar walks toward their future.

The royal family watched our progress from the choir. Among them was an elderly woman who appeared to be sobbing convulsively. We approached the high altar, where the splendidly arrayed archbishop of Canterbury waited with Arthur, prince of Wales. Arthur, too, was dressed all in white. He kept his eyes lowered. *Why does he not look at me?* A ripple of anxiety caused me to shiver.

My left hand, resting on Henry's right, had begun to tremble, and for a moment Henry's fingers gripped mine tightly. I sought his merry eye as he stepped aside to relinquish me to his brother, and I thought I heard him murmur "Catalina."

I moved stiffly through the many parts of the ceremony, aware of the blond boy kneeling at my side and sensing that his nervousness was even greater than my own. When the archbishop had pronounced the benediction over us, we rose from our knees and I lifted my veil—officially this time. My husband and I gazed at one another. *What is he thinking?* I wondered. Then Arthur smiled, and a wave of relief swept over me. *It is done,* I thought. *Nothing can go wrong now.*

We clasped hands eagerly and together began the great procession down the long aisle of the church and out into the street where bells pealed and more trumpet fanfares shattered the air.

Immediately, the duke of York appeared again by my side. "I am to escort you to the banquet at Bayard's Castle," he explained. "The prince is obliged to remain here at the cathedral to affix his seal to several documents."

"Harry," I said, as we made our way through the throngs, "please tell me: Who was the old woman who wept throughout the ceremony? She stood with your parents, and it seemed she never stopped sobbing."

Henry laughed heartily. "My father's mother, Lady Margaret. She always does that. She believes that every drop of happiness must be paid for with a cup of suffering and pain, and so when she is the happiest, she weeps the most." He looked at me and shrugged. "But do not be fooled by those tears and mistake them for softness. My grandmother is as strong as a suit of armor!"

Conduits of wine flowed freely in the streets of London for the enjoyment of the common people, while at Bayard's Castle the royal feasting began. I occupied the seat of honor on King Henry's right, with Ayala and Doña Elvira on the other side of me. Arthur's place was at a separate table with his brother and sisters. I found that odd. Should not my husband be at my side? Was this an English custom? When at last I managed to ask Ayala, he replied with a shrug, "The king's orders."

For several hours a parade of servitors presented a seemingly endless succession of dishes. Every creature that roamed the forests, swam the rivers, or flew across the sky appeared in some guise at the wedding feast: boar, venison, and rabbit; mutton and kid; trout, pike, carp, perch, eel, and sturgeon; crane, partridge, egret, peacock. Some creatures were stuffed and roasted; others were stewed, boiled, or preserved in a jelly. Between courses we marveled at elaborate warners and subtleties: towering creations of spun sugar depicting various scenes from the Bible and ancient mythology. Doña Elvira had instructed me to take only tiny tastes of each, but her advice was unnecessary. I was far too nervous to eat, thinking about the one more ceremony I had to endure.

Torches were lit around the Great Hall, and feasting gave way to dancing. My ladies again distinguished themselves as they executed our beautiful dances that bespoke of starry skies and abundant sunshine. Arthur led one of his aunts in a stately dance that I did not know, and I was well pleased by his gracefulness.

Then my new brother-in-law took as his partner his older sister, Princess Margaret, herself a skilled dancer. The two performed a lively dance that Henry contrived to make even livelier, entertaining the company with astonishing leaps and jumps, eventually casting off his surcoat and continuing to caper about in his doublet.

I was weary to the bone by the time it all ended in the small hours, but I knew this was only the beginning. The celebration would continue for ten days of feasting, dancing, and jousting. And now, before this night ended, I would have to submit to the part I had been dreading all along: the ceremony of the bedding.

CHAPTER 5

The Marriage Bed

Bayard's Castle, November 1501

W*hat is she like, York?" the prince asked the duke as they left the Great Hall after the wedding banquet. "You have spent more time with her than I have."*

"Very nice," Henry told his brother. "Intelligent, too. And comely, I should say."

Arthur sent him a sidelong glance. "Beautiful hair," he agreed. "But her gowns," he added dubiously. "Rather odd, do you not think?"

"I paid no attention to her gowns. I was too busy trying to make out what she was saying," Henry explained. "She is eloquent in Latin, but her pronunciation is difficult to understand. I have become skilled at speaking Latin her way. You will too, if you try."

"I wonder if she plays chess. It would give us a way to

pass the time at Ludlow. And do you happen to know if she sings well or plays an instrument? The virginals, for instance, or the lute? That might be pleasant on cold winter evenings."

"The princess did not speak of chess or music." Henry paused, helping his brother out of his ermine-trimmed robe and into the night robe that he was to wear for the next ceremony. "Is she going with you to Ludlow, then? I heard that her mother thinks you should not live together for a year or so. Queen Isabella wants to let her stay with Mother, the queen, and Grandmother to learn our language and the ways of our court."

Arthur frowned. "She is my wife now. She should be with me."

Henry said nothing, thinking how much he would enjoy having Arthur's comely new wife at court a while longer.

Arthur had begun to pace nervously. "Are you ready, Arthur?" Henry asked. "I am to escort you, and Buckingham will be with us. Brandon and many others are coming, too."

"I know that!" Arthur replied fretfully. He stopped pacing. His face was the color of ashes. "York, I am not sure about this—this bedding ceremony. I am not entirely clear on what is expected of me."

Henry's eyes widened with surprise. "Has Buckingham not instructed you? It is really just another ceremony, Arthur. Brandon has spoken to me of it. Something to be gotten over with. Nothing to worry about."

"Yes, I know what is supposed to happen. But what if it does not, quite? What if she—?" Arthur's voice faltered and failed. He sat down abruptly on a bench and covered his eyes with both hands.

Henry regarded his older brother benevolently. He even felt a little sorry for him. After a moment he tenderly grasped Arthur's hand and coaxed him to his feet. "Come, my lord of Wales, let us go now to the bedchamber. Your bride awaits you. Brandon says that even if it does not go just as you wish, all you need do is boast of it afterwards as though it did!"

Ever since Dogmersfield Doña Elvira had lectured me on many points regarding my wedding day, insisting especially that I must eat but little. "To evidence too much pleasure in the enjoyment of food would show you to be a person of appetites. That is unseemly for a highborn Spanish lady!"

This discourse on appetites led my duenna eventually to a much more detailed instruction on how I was to conduct myself on my wedding night.

My mother and I had had long talks about what I should expect in the marital bed. "What happens between a man and a woman is blessed by God and will lead in time to the begetting of offspring," she said—as though I did not know this, with three older sisters!— "but your father and I believe strongly that this should be delayed for a time, due to the youthful age of the prince and his delicate constitution."

My mother also made it clear that she did not wish me to accompany Arthur to Ludlow but preferred that I remain in London with the king and queen.

Doña Elvira supported my mother's view. "You have only to follow my instructions, and all will be well." But when I asked, she refused to tell me in advance what these instructions would be. "In due time," she said.

On our wedding night Arthur was escorted by the duke of York and the duke of Buckingham to his chambers and I to mine by the duchess of Norfolk and Princess Margaret and, of course, Doña Elvira. My ladies removed my robe, gown, and farthingale and replaced them with a delicately embroidered silken kirtle. Then my duenna took me aside and pressed into my hand a tiny bottle of venetian glass containing a dark liquid. "Take this with you, but conceal it well," she whispered.

Thinking it some potion that I was to swallow, perhaps to put me into a light slumber, I asked what it contained.

"Sheep's blood," she replied. "Before morning, make certain to spill a few drops upon the linen sheet. When the lords wish to see proof that your virginity was taken by the prince, this will be the evidence. But you need have no fear. I am assured that the prince has been directed by his father, the king, that the two of you are to live as brother and sister until some time in the future when it is deemed fitting for you to live as man and wife."

Arthur from his chamber and I from mine were then led to the nuptial chamber, already crowded with dignitaries, many of whom were merry with drink. The heavy damask bed curtains were drawn back, and the archbishop of Canterbury with great ceremony and many prayers and sprinkles of holy water blessed the bed upon which we were to lie. While Arthur's gentlemen guided him into the great bed from one side, my ladies helped me from the other. "Do not worry, Catalina," Francesca whispered. "It is the lot of women. Soon it will be over, and you will not mind at all."

"How would you know that, Francesca?" I asked, more sharply than intended due to my nervousness.

"So I have been told," she replied, blushing deeply and lowering her eyes. Perhaps, I thought, Doña Elvira was correct in saying that Francesca was lacking in shame.

The duke of Buckingham and Princess Margaret handed each of us a goblet containing spiced wine, which we sipped dutifully. The goblets were taken away, and Arthur and I lay down side by side, like the carved effigies on a royal tomb, still surrounded by lords and ladies of the court. Buckingham and the princess ceremoniously drew the bed curtains closed around us, and the revelers noisily withdrew from the bedchamber. The heavy door closed. We lay there listening as the raucous laughter gradually faded until all was quiet.

I clutched the glass vial in my left hand as Arthur reached for my right. He was trembling. Minutes passed. He sighed deeply. "Are you weary, dearest wife?" he asked at last.

"Quite weary, my lord."

"Perhaps, then, it would be wise to delay the conjugal act until another time?"

His question startled me, for I thought that decision had already been made. I was also not certain I understood him, for his Latin words were still strange to my ears. "As you wish, my lord," I replied.

Arthur shifted restlessly in the bed. "But it is the custom to show evidence of the act to the noblemen."

"I have the evidence here. My duenna gave it to me."

"You do?" Arthur rolled over onto his stomach. "What sort of evidence?"

"A vial of sheep's blood."

Arthur laughed with relief. "Splendid!" He patted my shoulder. "Then good night, dearest wife," he said. "Sleep well." Arthur turned away from me and curled up on his side.

I whispered, "Good night, beloved husband. God grant you a peaceful rest."

I tucked the glass vial between the mattresses, intending to follow Doña Elvira's instructions first thing in the morning. Soon Arthur was breathing deeply. Exhausted though I was, I could not sleep—not while this boy, this stranger, lay in the bed beside me, close enough to touch.

Arthur was still sleeping when a great clamor erupted outside our chamber the next morning. Doña Elvira's voice registered loud protest on the other side of the door, with even louder shouts and much boisterous laughter in reply.

"What can it be?" I asked Arthur, who was now fully awake and running his fingers through his thick blond curls.

"The lords of the bedchamber have come to greet us," he explained.

"This is an outrage!" my duenna shouted as the door burst open.

They paid her no attention. In a moment a dozen strangers had pulled back the bed curtains and gaped at us rudely. Behind them came musicians making all sorts of insufferable noises. There was much laughter and rough joking, and Arthur's fool pranced about, making comments that I was glad not to understand. So distressed was I by this intrusion that I burst into tears of shame. Under the coverlet Arthur squeezed my hand to comfort me and tried to explain that such was the custom here. I retorted that in my country such an invasion would be considered an insult.

This racket continued for some minutes. Arthur whispered to me, "Watch now. Here is my great pretense." He threw back the bedcovers, calling out in Latin in a great, boastful voice, "My friends, I believe that it is indeed a good pastime to have a wife!"

This remark was greeted with more laughter and all sorts of ill-mannered whistles and hoots. Stunned, I peered around for my duenna to come to my aid, but I soon found that she had swooned dead away and only halfhearted efforts were being made to revive her.

At the last moment I remembered the glass vial of sheep's blood hidden between the mattresses. While Arthur roistered with the gentlemen who laughed and joked with him, I pulled the cork stopper and, following my duenna's instructions, sprinkled a few drops of blood upon the spotless white linen sheet.

For a fortnight the celebrations continued—pageants and tournaments, feasting and dancing, masquing and disguising, gambling at cards and at dice—and so did the debate about whether I should accompany my husband to Ludlow and begin to share his life or whether I should remain with the royal court in London. On the thirtieth of November the celebrations came to an end; I learned that the first portion of my dowry—100,000 escudos—had been handed over by the ambassador to King Henry, and my household and I were moved to Richmond Palace, the king's favorite.

I understood that Arthur needed to return to Ludlow to resume his duties as prince of Wales. I also understood that I was too young and possibly too delicate to take up life in that wild, rough country. Doña Elvira insisted that I must not go, that she had given her word to my mother I would not. "Perhaps in a year," she said.

But my chaplain, Padre Alessandro, insisted just as strongly that I must go now.

I felt myself pulled first one way and then the other and sometimes wept with perplexity and bafflement. It was not my choice to make, and just as well, for I would not have known how to make it. "The king will decide," I reminded my duenna and my chaplain. "Neither you nor I have a voice."

At last Arthur sent me a message: King Henry had decided that the prince of Wales must return to Ludlow before the start of Yuletide and that I was to accompany him. Padre Alessandro smiled benevolently while Doña Elvira raged, but she could not defy the orders of the English king. Early in December, I prepared to make another journey, this time with my husband to my new home in Wales.

CHAPTER 6

The Longest Season

Eltham Palace, January 1502

henry watched as the great procession—*Arthur's knights and priests and henchmen and the princess's Spanish retinue, carts and mules laden with their belongings, the princess closed in her litter and Arthur on horseback*—set off from Richmond Palace, wound through the hills, and finally disappeared into the forest.

After the excitement of the wedding, he was sorry to see them leave. He had grown fond of the princess and of his role as her escort and the attention it brought him. If Catherine had remained at court, he believed there was much he could have taught her: to speak French fluently; to dance in the English manner; to play upon the lute, if she did not know how; and to sing some pretty songs. Perhaps he could have taught her to speak English as well.

"Why do you not stay at Richmond for Yuletide?" Henry had asked Arthur, who shrugged and replied, *"Father, the king, wishes me to be in the Welsh Marches by Christmas."* And that was that.

After Twelfth Night the duke and his sisters returned by royal barge to Eltham Palace near Greenwich with its great hunting park, fine banqueting halls, and puppet theater. Henry had spent the past ten years at Eltham under the care of various nursemaids, governors, and tutors. He resumed his studies under the direction of his principal tutor, John Skelton, who had been chosen by Lady Margaret.

His days began long before the sun rose. Henry shivered sleepily through matins sung by his chaplain, and at six o'clock stumbled to the chapel royal to hear daily mass. He was always ravenous by the first meal of the day, gulping down a flagon of ale and devouring the bread and meat set out for him in his chambers.

The intellectually rigorous mornings ground by: Latin and Greek, followed by French and penmanship lessons, and later, under Skelton's demanding eye, on to mathematics, logic, and law. His tutors agreed that Henry was a gifted student, and Erasmus, the renowned humanist scholar who came from Amsterdam to visit the Tudor court that winter, pronounced him "brilliant."

By dinnertime, after the morning lessons, Henry was again famished. Liveried servants presented the dishes and Skelton presided at table with a stout stick, whacking Henry's knuckles when the duke forgot himself and wiped his greasy hands on his doublet.

Once dinner was finished, Henry could scarcely wait to be away from his books and out into the park. Brandon often waited for him, challenging him to a sword fight, a footrace, a contest of some kind. He could run faster than the cousins who often joined them. He leaped easily over ditches and fences, leaving the others far behind, except for Brandon who always won.

*By four o'clock darkness was closing in, and even Henry was ready to leave the park for the warmth of a blazing fire. Supper, taken with good appetite, was followed by evening prayers, in which he never failed to mention the members of the royal family by name, beginning with his grandmother, Lady Margaret, and now including Catherine, princess of Wales. Arthur was so fortunate to have married such an appealing wife—and intelligent as well! Henry thought often of the Spanish princess—*Catalina, a pretty name—*wondering how she fared at Ludlow with dear, dull Arthur. She would have a merrier time of it if he, Henry, were there.*

Weary at last, he retired to his bedchamber, bade Brandon a good night, and fell into a deep and untroubled sleep.

Early in December we made our farewells to King Henry and Queen Elizabeth and the rest of the family and set out from Richmond. The duke of York put on a great show of his good-bye, telling me that I must say *au revoir,* thus adding another French phrase to my small vocabulary.

Days before our departure, many of my countrymen prepared to return to Spain—not only the bishops and titled gentlemen, but also the trumpeters, cooks, servers, and others who had been sent to assist with the wedding. How it saddened me to see them leave! A part of my heart went with them.

Some sixty Spaniards remained with me in England. Doña Elvira hovered close by, murmuring words of encouragement when I needed them, or relentlessly enforcing rules she insisted had been laid down by my mother, which I could not disprove. How much she annoyed me! But I could not argue with her, for though I had been well schooled in obedience, I had not yet learned to assert myself.

Doña Elvira's husband, Don Pedro Manrique, served as my majordomo, in charge of my household. Their son, Iñigo, tall and gaunt as his mother, silent as his father, was my equerry, charged with the care of our horses and mules. Padre Alessandro heard my confessions and said mass for us. My fools, Santiago and Urraca, did their best to amuse me, and the minstrels, however downcast they may have felt, were ready to strum us a merry tune whenever we stopped to rest. And my ladies! I could not have done without Maria, Inez, and Francesca, always present to soothe and encourage me, no matter how much they suffered from the strange food and foul weather.

The air had turned sharply colder since my arrival in England, and I traveled inside the royal litter, bundled in furs, sometimes cupping my hands over my nose to warm it. My ladies, who took turns riding in the litter with me, and our maidservants all complained of the icy winds. The English appeared undisturbed by the cold that found its way into our very bones. Even Arthur, who was not robust, seemed not to mind spending the day on horseback, regardless of the elements. Francesca shivered and wept, crying that her tears turned to ice on her cheeks. I wondered myself how I would endure the long winter, but I tried to put on a cheerful face for my new husband, to hide from him my discomfort.

The farther we traveled to the north and west, the wilder the countryside became. We were bound for the Marches, the borderland between England and Wales. Centuries before, a line of heavily fortified castles had been built along that border as a defense against the barbarian hordes to the west. Now one of these ancient castles would be my home.

I understood little of what was expected of Arthur, except that this was the far edge of England, that the Welsh were an unruly lot, and Arthur's presence was expected to help maintain peace and order. Perhaps, I thought, I might be of help to him in this, for I was accustomed to the way my parents always worked together as a team to unite the peoples of Aragon and Castilla.

Along our route the good country people turned out to cheer us, skin reddened and noses dripping. We made stops at several great manor houses, property of the prince of Wales, and I passed my sixteenth birthday at Bewdley, where a special feast had been prepared in my honor.

To the table that night servitors carried one of the strangest dishes I had ever seen. The forward half of a suckling pig had been stitched to the rear half of a capon, the remaining back half of the piglet stitched to the front end of the capon, both creatures then stuffed with a mixture of bread and eggs and roasted upon a spit. Gilded with gold foil and accompanied by blaring trumpets, this creation, called a cockentrice, was presented upon silver platters, as though it were the most marvelous dish in the world.

I stole a glance at Doña Elvira, who looked as though she might faint at the sight of it. *"¡Qué horror!"* she muttered. Even the hardy Padre Alessandro looked a little squeamish.

The cockentrice aside, I wished we could have stayed on at Bewdley, set in the midst of a lovely park close by the gentle Severn River. Knowing that was impossible, I hoped Ludlow's castle would turn out to be as charming as the Bewdley manor.

When we arrived at Ludlow, I was most disappointed. Surrounded by a deep moat, the ancient castle loomed forbiddingly over the village. Arthur proudly led me through a gate in the curtain wall, thicker than the height of a man, across an open space to an inner wall, and through yet another portal to the inner bailey. Though I thought the castle grim from the outside, I found the inside to be more cheerful. Fires blazed in enormous hearths, colorful tapestries warmed the rough stone walls, and candles brightened the dark chambers. Arthur and his gentlemen escorted me to my apartments with great ceremony. When he had left me for his own apartments in another part of the castle, I inspected the bed with its several mattresses stuffed with wool and the rich tapestries that enclosed it and pronounced it satisfactory. Doña Elvira sniffed, glaring her general disapproval, but ordered our goods unpacked.

"I shall be able to sleep well enough here, I suppose," she said.

I could not conceal my surprise. "In my chamber, Doña Elvira?"

"As your esteemed parents, the kings of Spain, have instructed," she said in a tone that allowed no argument.

Once more I chose to keep silent rather than challenge my duenna. When I think back upon it now, I wonder at how meekly I accepted her assertion that my parents had ordered it. Had they really told her that she must sleep with me even after I became a wife? Whether they had or not, I decided that surely it was my husband's obligation to tell her otherwise. But, to be truthful, I felt more relief than disappointment, for I was not eager for Arthur to begin visits to my bed that must inevitably end in "the conjugal act," as he called it.

We had arrived at Ludlow the week before the feast of the Nativity. My first Yuletide spent away from home in a strange land was part heartache and part enchantment for me. The wild-haired, bearded Welsh chieftains came to our banquets dressed in leather and sheepskin rather than silk and velvet, to pay their respects to their young prince and to me, his bride. They brought with them harpists and other musicians, and after the feasting ended they would stay until the small hours of the morning, drinking great flagons of ale, singing their dirgelike tunes, and reciting the story of their misty past in long poems. Though I understood not a single word of their language, which sounded even more strange to my ears than did English, I loved the rolling cadences of their voices.

Often, I called upon my minstrels to entertain our guests with songs from Spain that gladdened my heart but at the same time filled it with longing. On the eve of Christmas Francesca reminded me of the tiny oil lamps that were lighted in the windows of every home, from castle to cottage, to welcome the Christ child. And then Maria began to speak of the delicious cakes made of almonds and honey and scented with lemons. I could almost taste them. Nothing is so wrenching as thoughts of one's old life at Yuletide, and these tender memories set us to weeping.

Then Inez, always practical, scolded us. "That was our old life," she said. "This is our new one."

"Indulge us a little, dear Inez," I begged her. "You are right, but that does not lessen our yearning."

During this tranquil season, Arthur sometimes conducted me to various parts of the rambling old castle, so that I might become familiar with my home and its long history. During our walks he described to me life at his father's court, sometimes adding, "When I am king and you are my queen, we shall do the same."

Each New Year's morning, Arthur told me, he and his brother and sisters were summoned to the king's bedchamber, where they watched silently as their father received gifts from every member of his court according to rank, from highest to lowest. Next, his mother entered the chamber and received her gifts in the same manner.

"I was third," Arthur said. "And then York. After that, my sisters. Little Mary was always the last to see her gifts, and by then the poor thing was so exhausted she could scarcely mumble thanks. Perhaps that is a custom we could change."

"Gifts on New Year's Day?" I asked, explaining that in Spain we exchanged gifts on the Feast of the Three Kings, the sixth of January.

"The sixth of January is known as Twelfth Night," Arthur said, "an occasion for merrymaking. Sometimes the revelers drink too much ale. You may not find it to your liking, Catherine."

Catherine. Not Catalina. Members of my Spanish retinue continued to call me Catalina, but to my husband I had a different name. Slowly my ear was growing accustomed to the way Arthur spoke Latin, and his to mine, so that our conversations flowed more easily. But I was still not used to being called Catherine.

Twelfth Night arrived. Sir Richard Pole, the prince's chamberlain, carried a brimming bowl of spiced ale into the Great Hall of the castle, crying "Wassail! Wassail!" (I learned that it means "Good health!") A little band of minstrels and choristers played and sang, the ale was drunk—I merely pretended—and the feasting began. "Shield of brawn" was served, boar meat steeped in vinegar. The English consumed it with gusto, but it proved too strong for my stomach. I felt quite ill afterwards and retired early to my chambers. Thus I was not present when the feasting turned to drunkenness, though I heard whispers for days afterward of mildly improper behavior.

Twelfth Night marked the end of Yuletide, and Arthur returned to his regular duties, meeting with the council that the king had appointed to help him govern. I saw little of him during those busy days, but I had the good fortune to make the acquaintance of Lady Margaret Pole, wife of Sir Richard. Lady Margaret was several years older than I, a handsome woman, both elegant and dignified. She was also pious, which I appreciated greatly, and interested in books and literature.

I passed my days in conversation with Lady Margaret, with whom I spoke Latin, or with my ladies as we sat with our needlework in our laps. My mother had insisted that my sisters and I learn to sew a fine seam. She had always stitched my father's shirts, and it seemed fitting that I would do the same for my husband. I had my fools to amuse me, and through the long, dark evenings the minstrels played for us. When the Welshmen came, as they often did, we listened to the music of their poetry.

We served frequent banquets, which often left my stomach unwell for days. I found English food nearly unpalatable and longed for the luscious fruits—the rosy pomegranates and juicy oranges and plump figs—fresh from the trees of my homeland. And I thought the English banquets curious in the way the dozens of dishes, carried in by servitors, were always presented in a particular order. Crane arrived first, followed by heron; rabbit was always served after pigeon, not before. No one could explain why this was the case.

"A matter of tradition, my lady princess," Lady Margaret informed me when I asked.

It was not my place to interfere with tradition, but I did let it be known that I hoped the dreadful cockentrice would not appear at any future banquets.

Slowly, Arthur and I learned to know each other. I taught him card games that I once played with my brother and sisters. Arthur began to teach me to play chess. I enjoyed the time we spent together, and my fondness for Arthur grew. Late in January I wrote to my sister, Juana, with whom I had always felt close: *On days when the sun surprises us with a rare appearance, we wrap ourselves in furs and ride our mounts along the banks of the River Teme and the River Corve. Someday I hope that you and Philip might visit us here.*

Every evening after prayers when it was time to retire, Arthur kissed my hand. "Sleep well, dear wife," he said. "May angels watch over you until the morrow." Then he kissed my hand again, and we retired to our separate chambers.

There were occasional nights, though, when I was startled awake by a page, announcing in a loud voice that the prince wished to visit my bedchamber. The page then dismissed the protesting Doña Elvira "by order of His Majesty, the prince of Wales."

I leaped out of my bed and knelt upon the frigid stone floor, shivering in my silken shift, until Arthur arrived, took me by my cold hand, and led me into the bed. There we lay side by side, our hands touching, and Arthur told me of a troubling dream from which he had awakened, frightened and unable to fall asleep again.

"Dear Catherine, can you tell me the meaning of this dream?" he would ask.

I listened quietly. I was not an interpreter of dreams, but I asked him a few questions and tried to re-assure him that the dream did not seem to me to pose any threat. Sometimes, thus comforted, he would drift into a peaceful sleep while I lay motionless in order not to disturb him—and thus sleepless myself. The affection I felt for Arthur deepened, like a sister's love for a beloved brother, like the love I had had for Juan.

I remained a virgin.

CHAPTER 7

Death in Springtime

Eltham Palace, February 1502

The duke of York, weighted down by helmet and breast-plate and cuisses strapped to his thighs, ran heavily toward the galloping horse, its gray mane streaming. When the gelding came within reach, Henry seized a handful of the mane and lunged, attempting to leap into the saddle without the use of stirrups. But the horse veered sharply away, tearing the long, rough hairs from Henry's grasp. Thrown off balance, the boy staggered and collapsed onto the frozen ground in a clattering heap of metal. He heard Brandon's laughter—Brandon, who could vault onto the back of a galloping horse from any angle!

The duke's riding master caught the gelding by the bridle. "Once more, my lord," he called out, preparing to send the horse flying again toward Henry.

His labored breath turning to frosty clouds, Henry struggled to his feet and braced himself as the horse raced toward him. This time the horse came on straightaway, but too fast. Brandon's taunting laughter echoing in his ears, Henry gathered all his strength and made a desperate leap. Without stirrups to assist him, he landed in the saddle with a grunt, off balance, but he managed to keep his seat and to seize the reins and slow the horse to a trot.

"An improvement," called the riding master, taking the reins. "Once again, my lord!"

On his third attempt the duke heard Brandon's hearty cheer and knew that this time all had gone as it should. He waited for words of praise from the riding master, but they were not forthcoming. They seldom were. "Now we shall practice mounting from the opposite side, my lord."

In a few days Henry and his household would return to Richmond for Shrovetide, before the start of Lent. There would be feasting, of course, and also jousting—running at the rings, at which Henry was accomplished, and tilting. Henry was fearless. He was certain that he would charge straight at his opponent, his lance held steady, and unhorse him. He wished that Arthur and Catherine might be present to witness this display of skill, but the king had said it was too soon for the prince and princess to come back from Ludlow. "At Eastertide, York," he had answered shortly, when Henry asked.

He was surprised by how much he missed Arthur and his bride. When the prince and princess were there, the king paid less attention to Henry. On the whole that was a good thing, for it meant his father found less fault with him. Henry believed he was the least favored of his father's children. Arthur, of course, was the heir. His sisters would make political marriages arranged with men whose families were important allies. But Henry had not yet learned what his father planned for his future. He knew that his grandmother wished him to become a priest and one day to serve as archbishop of Canterbury, the most important position in the church. But he had heard his father tell Lady Margaret, "The duke will be more useful to me in Flanders or Austria than in the pulpit." His father's wishes would prevail, he was certain of that, and he hoped that when a bride was found for him, she would be as pleasing as Princess Catherine.

As THE DAYS OF WINTER PASSED, THE WINDS HOWLED around Ludlow's massive stone towers, sleet tapped insistently at the windows, and snow piled in billowing drifts around the castle like a mantle of ermine. After such a storm had lasted for days, the skies suddenly cleared. That night Arthur summoned me to walk out with him in the snow-covered bailey.

"You must not even consider such a foolhardy act," said Doña Elvira sternly.

"But my husband wishes it," I replied.

"Your husband in name only." Her jaw was set, her voice wintry. "It is my sworn duty to protect you from just such folly. And I always do my duty, as must you, Catalina."

Her stubborn insistence only hardened my determination. "And my duty, Doña Elvira, is to my lawful husband," I said, emphasizing the words.

Shutting my ears to Doña Elvira's dire warnings of certain illness, I called for my maidservants to pull on my leather boots and ran out to meet him. The stars shone brightly, and the snow gleamed silver in the moonlight. I believed I had never seen anything so beautiful.

Hand in hand Arthur and I trudged happily through knee-deep snow across the inner bailey toward the Round Chapel of Saint Mary Magdalene. Ours were the only tracks in the fresh snow. When we reached the chapel, Arthur pushed open the heavy door, and like naughty children we crept inside. A few moonbeams poured through the narrow windows and splashed on the stone floor. Arthur smiled and laid his finger to his lips, signing me not to speak. I realized that the ladies and gentlemen who always accompanied us were nowhere to be seen. For a rare moment we were alone.

Arthur turned to me and took me awkwardly in his arms for the first time. He pressed his cold mouth against mine. I had never before been kissed upon my lips, and I eagerly welcomed his embrace. But before I could return the kiss, Arthur pulled away from me abruptly and broke into a hacking cough. The fit went on and on. Its severity frightened me.

We stumbled out of the inky shadows of the chapel and into the wintry night. Arthur coughed again, bent over at the waist, and I stared in horror at the spatters of blood that bloomed like holly berries in the pristine snow.

"My husband," I gasped in alarm. "You are ill!"

"It is nothing," Arthur muttered. He seized my hand and hurried me back to the castle. "Speak no more of it," he said.

I longed to tell someone—Doña Elvira, Lady Margaret Pole, anyone—but I said nothing, though I was deeply troubled. If he learned I had spoken of the incident, our fragile trust would be broken. But how ill *was* he? Even as I worried, I thought again and again of Arthur's kiss. It had seemed to signal a change since our marriage three months earlier. But the kiss had been ended abruptly—was that also a sign?

Soon after that night in the snow, my fears were realized, and Arthur took to his bed. For a fortnight apothecaries administered potions made of herbs, and after much consultation, the physicians bled him. In time he seemed to recover and was up and about and again tending to the business of governing. Yet I could see that he had lost strength. His pallor was alarming. He complained to me that his cough kept him awake at night, but he said nothing about the blood, and I dared not ask.

The days passed as steadily and inexorably as the rain that dripped from the tree branches and froze in sparkling fingers of ice. My hands and face grew chapped and raw from the cold and dampness. Lady Margaret recommended that I apply goose fat to soften and heal them. This good woman had other advice for me: that I must learn to speak a little English.

"It will serve you well with the common people, who speak no Latin," she advised, and sometimes as we sat at our stitching she tutored me in the new language: *Hail. Farewell. If it please you. Cup. Bowl. Needle. Thread. Table.*

I longed for spring. I worried about Arthur. My sister, Juana, wrote from Flanders that she was expecting another child. I sent long letters to my parents and yearned for some word from them but received none. My mother had warned me that letters often took weeks, even months, to reach their destination, and so I was not troubled much by their silence.

Rain. Snow. Sun. Moon. Clouds.

The ladies of my court could not abide Ludlow, though mostly they managed to conceal their discontent. Only Francesca occasionally lost patience. "I miss Spain so much I wish I could die!" she cried out on one occasion, and my heart echoed her words. But Maria chastised her and urged her to be brave "for the sake of our lady princess."

I watched Arthur carefully. He looked weary, I thought, and his face had grown gaunt. He lacked the strength to walk about in the countryside with me or to ride to a nearby village, even when we were favored with a rare mild day. When I finally collected the courage to mention this to Lady Margaret, she brushed aside my concerns. "Once fair weather arrives, your husband is sure to grow robust again," she said. But I thought I detected an unease beneath her cheerful assurances.

On Shrove Tuesday, the last great feast before the beginning of Lent, Arthur felt strong enough to enjoy a banquet before we plunged into the unremitting gloom of the penitential season: forty days of fasting and prayer. My fool, Santiago, entertained us with his tumbling and grotesque dances, disappearing and reappearing in ever more eccentric costumes. The minstrels played, my ladies and I danced, we drank wine and feasted. I observed that Arthur had little appetite, and my worries about him increased tenfold.

The next day, Ash Wednesday, marked the beginning of Lent. I packed away my jewels, intending not to wear them until the festal season of Easter. That evening we ate only a small supper of bread and water. Doña Elvira vowed to continue this sacrifice through the entire Lenten fast.

My chaplain, Padre Alessandro, believed such an austere diet was an unnecessary penance for me and urged me to eat a little salt fish and whatever vegetables had lasted through the winter. According to the cook, these were mainly turnips.

Arthur visited me only once in my bedchamber during those somber days. "I dreamed that Death, dressed in a long red cloak, had come for me," he told me, holding my hand in both of his.

"Are you certain that it was Death?" I asked him. "I believe that Death wears black, or perhaps white. But not red."

I had no notion if what I said were true, but the idea seemed to comfort Arthur. "You are a good wife to me," he murmured and fell into a light sleep broken by a fit of coughing that drove him from my bed. After he had gone, I searched for telltale droplets of blood on the pillow and was relieved to find none. Still, I wondered if the red of the cloak in Arthur's dream signified blood. Again I felt weak with fear for our future.

The prince's visit earned me the disapproval of my duenna. "A Christian gentleman does not visit his wife's bed during the period of Lent," she lectured me sternly.

I merely nodded. "He visits *me,* not my bed," I told her, "as is his right as well as mine." I did not mention his fright or the dream that had induced it.

"Such impertinence does not become you, Catalina," said Doña Elvira, but she did not speak further of Arthur's visit.

The weeks passed. As the days began to lengthen, my hopes rose. "Soon it will be Easter," I reminded my ladies in an effort to cheer them.

On the morning of Palm Sunday Arthur ordered that bare branches be cut from the copper beeches surrounding the castle and carried in procession in honor of our Lord's entry into Jerusalem. On Maundy Thursday, following tradition, the prince of Wales washed the feet of several of the servants of the castle, as our Lord did with his disciples before breaking bread with them for the last time. On Good Friday we fasted and spent the hours of Christ's suffering upon our knees in the chapel. The Great Vigil, the first service of Easter day, commenced at midnight Saturday with the lighting of the paschal candle. Mass was followed by a banquet. When it all ended, I was stumbling with fatigue, and I saw that Arthur looked much paler and weaker than usual.

"Are you unwell, my lord?" I asked him uneasily.

He shook his head and made no reply. *Why does he not answer me?* I wondered. *Why does he not tell me if he is ill?*

Just as the first warm breaths of air stirred the still-bare branches and the sun appeared for whole minutes at a time, I was taken with an ague. For more than a fortnight I burned with fever and shivered with cold. My whole body ached, and my head ached even more. Doña Elvira had left my chambers to order a poultice prepared for me when one of the royal physicians brought word that my husband had fallen desperately ill again.

"There is grievous concern for his life," said the physician somberly.

"For his life?" I cried. "Why am I being told of this only now?"

"Because madam's health has not permitted it," said the physician. "And there was still hope for the prince's recovery."

"There is no longer hope of that?" I threw aside the coverlet and called for a maidservant to bring me a robe to cover my shift. "I shall go to him at once," I said.

Despite my feverish weakness, I rushed barefoot through the freezing gallery from my chambers to Arthur's. *My husband, dying! Surely not! Oh, if it please God, surely not!*

I arrived to find the prince, my husband, surrounded by his physicians in their furred gowns, his apothecaries preparing herbs, his astrologers consulting their charts, and his chaplains muttering prayers. I tried to push my way through this crowd to my husband's side, but I was held back, gently but firmly, by Arthur's chamberlain, Sir Richard Pole.

"But I must go to him!" I cried, struggling to break free. "Arthur needs me. I know that I can comfort him!"

"There is nothing more to be done for him, madam," whispered the chamberlain. "The prince is gravely ill and no longer in possession of his senses. It is my painful duty to tell you, my lady princess, that he may not last the night. There is nothing left for us but to pray."

I fell to my knees upon the cold stone floor near Arthur's bed and began to pray fervently. My prayers were interrupted when Doña Elvira burst into the chambers, her sleeping garments in disarray, and demanded to know what I was doing there.

"I am with my husband," I said, in as firm a voice as I could muster. "The prince is dying," I added, and these words seemed to cause the duenna to quiet herself. She, too, knelt with others of the household who gathered hastily. As the hours passed I remained upon my knees, offering the discomfort of my body as a sacrifice. Padre Alessandro stayed by my side, comforting me, leading me in prayers first for God's healing grace upon my suffering husband and then, as dawn approached, in prayers for the repose of the soul of Arthur, prince of Wales.

Arthur was dead. With Sir Richard and Padre Alessandro supporting me, I made my way to Arthur's bed and kissed him. It was only our second kiss, and our last.

Arms lifted and carried me to my own chamber, placing me in my own bed. For several days I drifted in and out of awareness. Compresses were laid upon my forehead, poultices upon my chest. Leeches were placed upon my arms to bleed me, and clysters were administered. Each time that I awakened from merciful sleep, I realized afresh that my husband was dead, and I was a widow, all alone in a new world still completely strange to me. *What would happen to me now?* The enormity of that question plunged me again into whirling darkness.

Arthur died on the second day of April *anno Domini* 1502. What I remember of the next month I learned because it was told to me by others—Doña Elvira, Margaret Pole, and Padre Alessandro.

My husband's body lay in state in the Great Hall of Ludlow Castle for nearly three weeks, surrounded by blazing torches and dozens of candles. High-ranking noblemen journeyed from all over England to pay their final respects to the dead prince.

Maria de Salinas, her eyes swollen with tears, whispered to me that plans had been made to remove the body from Ludlow Castle to the parish church, where a requiem mass would be sung on the twenty-third of April, Saint George's Day, an occasion deeply observed in England. I was still very weak, but I had not yet said my private farewells to my dead husband. Knowing that Doña Elvira, in her ceaseless efforts to protect me, would do all in her power to prevent me, I asked Maria to arrange to have me carried into the Great Hall in secret, when the duenna was asleep. The loyal Maria promised to stay with me by Arthur's coffin while I bade him a last farewell.

Two servants, accompanied by Maria and Padre Alessandro, came for me sometime after midnight. For a little while I knelt by the coffin, my hand on the black velvet pall. "Until we meet again in heaven, dear husband," I whispered and bent forward to kiss the carved wooden lid.

Later, as once again I lay in my bed, gray dawn streaked the sky beyond my narrow window. Maria lay beside me, stroking my hand and softly murmuring words of comfort. Doña Elvira had already begun to stir on the other side of the bed curtains.

Several more days had passed when Padre Alessandro visited me and described the funeral. "The coffin was carried to the parish church in a procession lit by smoking torches. After the requiem mass, Arthur's heart was buried in the churchyard. I witnessed that myself."

Later still, Lady Margaret sat by my side as I lay there, still too weak to leave my bed, and continued the story. Her husband, Sir Richard, had accompanied the funeral cortege on its long journey through wind and rain to Worcester Cathedral; oxen were needed to pull the hearse along rutted roads deep with mud. On Saint Mark's Day, the twenty-fifth of April, Arthur's coffin was lowered into the grave. The officers of the household broke their rods of office and cast the broken pieces down upon the lid of the coffin, and the earth closed upon it forever.

CHAPTER 8

Mourning

Eltham Palace, April 1502

"**B**uckingham is here." *Henry, playing tennis with Brandon, recognized the duke's black and red livery and laid aside his racquet. He wondered at the unusually small retinue—only half a dozen gentlemen. Buckingham never traveled so lightly.*

The two waited as the group approached. Buckingham swung down from the saddle and dropped to his knees. "My lord," said the duke in a choked voice.

Henry frowned. "What is it, Buckingham?"

"Arthur is dead!" he cried. "My lord, your brother, the prince of Wales, has departed this mortal life. Your father and mother have given me the terrible duty of bringing you this dreadful news."

*Numbly, Henry stared at him. "Arthur is dead?" he re-
peated. "My brother has died? But when? How?" His
knees began to tremble so violently that he felt as though he
might topple over.*

*Buckingham described what little he knew: Consump-
tion, though it might have been the sweating sickness. Four
days past, on the second of April. Henry struggled to absorb
these facts, despite the roaring in his ears.*

*"Your father, the king, has ordered me to bring you to
him at Richmond," Buckingham said.*

*The duke of York and his sisters had returned to
Eltham just days earlier, after a quiet Easter spent at
Greenwich. Arthur and Princess Catherine had not come
from Ludlow after all, sending word that both were too ill
to make the journey. The king and queen had worried—
unlike Henry, Arthur always suffered from a weak constitution—but no one had been prepared for the arrival of
the exhausted courier dispatched by Sir Richard Pole to inform King Henry and Queen Elizabeth of the death of
their eldest child. Hours later, Buckingham had left for
Eltham.*

*Slowly, the two walked toward the palace where
Henry had spent most of his boyhood. Brandon trailed behind, lost in thought. At this moment the reality of Arthur's
death found its way into Henry's heart, and he broke into
sobs that shook his body from crown to sole. Brandon
stepped forward, wrapped his strong arms around the weeping boy, and held him against his great chest. For a time,*

Henry allowed himself to be comforted, soothed by the steady drumbeat of Brandon's heart.

When he was calm again and orders had been given to prepare for his departure for Richmond, Henry thought to ask about Catherine. Buckingham could tell him little, except that though the princess of Wales, too, was ill, she was, the last he heard, still alive.

Later, as the royal barge carried Henry and his company up the Thames toward Richmond, a thought—shameful but at the same time deeply thrilling—stole into Henry's mind: Now, I shall become the prince of Wales. And someday I shall be king!

SPRING CREPT OVER THE SORROWING LAND. TREES leafed out nearly overnight, flowers bloomed everywhere in profuse defiance of our burden of grief, birds took up cheerful songs that were insults to our ears, and the month of May was half over when my physicians determined that I was well enough to undertake the long journey to London.

I said my good-byes to Lady Margaret, Sir Richard, and other members of Arthur's household and left Ludlow. Despite her woe, Queen Elizabeth had showed great consideration, sending me her own mourning litter draped in black velvet to ease my travel. Accompanied by the members of my own household, I slowly retraced the steps of the journey I had made six months earlier as Arthur's bride. When we stopped to rest in Bewdley where I had celebrated my sixteenth birthday in December, my heart ached with the bitterness of my unhappy situation.

"What does my future hold for me?" I wept despairingly to my ladies. "Where will I go? What will I do?"

"Whatever happens, we are with you, my lady," Maria assured me.

"You are our lady princess," said Inez, "and we shall not leave you."

I knew that I had no choice in the matter, nothing at all to say about my future. That would be decided by my parents and by King Henry, without consulting my wishes. I remembered when my oldest sister, Isabel, had been widowed. I was there when she was brought back from Portugal, grief-stricken after the death of her husband in a hunting accident. She was determined to spend the rest of her days in a convent.

My mother would not hear of it. "The duty of the daughter of the royal houses of Spain," she told my sister, "is to make a marriage that strengthens the bonds of those houses." At the end of her mourning period, Isabel was sent back to Portugal to marry the uncle of her dead husband. That was her duty. But what was mine?

In time my parents would choose a new husband for me. I had no idea who that person would be or what I was to do until that time arrived. Though I wanted nothing more than to return to Spain, for the present I must await word from my parents.

When I arrived in London after the slow, sorrowful journey from Ludlow, the king ordered me sent to Durham House, a vast London mansion. Handsome marble pillars lined the stately halls. Lovely gardens, filled with bountiful bloom, stretched down to the banks of the Thames. Durham House was much more to my liking than bleak Ludlow.

I had scarcely arrived in London when I discovered

that I had not been named heir to my husband's worldly goods, as I had assumed I would be. All of Prince Arthur's jewels and plate and furs had become the property of his father, the king. I thought it odd, yet at the time this did not trouble me unduly. Eventually I would receive a portion of the revenues from Wales and other districts, as agreed upon in the marriage treaty signed years earlier, and I trusted that King Henry would assume responsibility for my support in the meantime. I put the matter out of my mind.

Nearly all of my English servants had resigned at the time of Arthur's death, and my retinue now numbered sixty Spaniards. Doña Elvira promptly took over the task of organizing my household, assigning chambers, and arranging my possessions, some of which had not been unpacked since my arrival in England. Among the items were several chests of gold and silver plate, as well as jewels, representing a portion of my dowry still owed to King Henry. Doña Elvira saw no reason not to use the platters, ewers, flagons, and goblets in my newly established lodgings. But when Juan de Cuero, my household treasurer, learned of her plans, he refused to allow it.

"These items are part of the princess's dowry," he insisted. "They are not for Princess Catalina's use."

"Nonsense," snapped Doña Elvira. "The prince is dead, and the rules no longer apply."

But Cuero was adamant, and the two argued about the matter, loudly and often. This was but the first of the feuds to break out in my household. Having no idea who was right, I begged them to forget their differences. In the end, Cuero kept the upper hand.

Whether or not I could use my plate was of less importance to me than what I soon discovered about Durham. Though elegant, the mansion was just as cold and damp as Ludlow. On the coldest, wettest days, a fire blazed in the Great Hall, but my own chambers had no hearth. Instead, a fire-pan was filled with hot coals and wheeled to where it was needed. Though it was now June—glorious springtime in Spain—my hands were sometimes so cold that I could scarcely hold a spoon.

My first official call after I reached London and had settled into Durham House was to my mother-in-law, Queen Elizabeth, at Richmond Palace. She was in deep mourning, as was I, and the two of us embraced and wept together. I had liked the queen from the first and believed her motto well suited her: "Humble and Reverent." To that I would have added "Kind."

The queen and I spoke together quietly. Then she said gently, "It would give us a measure of joy in the midst of our sorrow, dear lady princess, to learn that you are with child."

I lowered my eyes, feeling so abashed that I was unable to meet her expectant gaze. "No, madam," I replied, "I am not. It is not possible."

"Not possible?"

"Our marriage was not consummated," I whispered, my face hot with shame to be discussing such matters.

"Ah," she sighed, wiping away another tear, "I had hoped otherwise. It has been my greatest wish that Arthur left us an heir."

Sighing deeply, the queen beckoned me to stand by her side at a window overlooking a courtyard. As I joined her at the window, I caught sight of my husband's younger brother, whom I had not seen since Arthur and I left for the Welsh Marches in December. Henry was now nearly eleven, a strapping young lad who seemed from this vantage to have grown even taller.

"All hopes now rest upon the duke of York," said the queen. "We have lost three sons—Edmund died before he reached his second birthday, another babe did not live to his christening, and now Arthur. An infant daughter left us as well."

His mother and I watched, side by side, as Henry's friend, Charles Brandon, engaged him in a wrestling match. Brandon was several years older than Henry, closer to my age than to York's, yet the young duke nearly overpowered him. In a few years' time Brandon would doubtless find himself on the losing end of these matches.

"I will share a secret with you, dear Catherine," the queen whispered so that her ladies would not hear, "and it is for your ears alone. Not a word to anyone, do you understand?"

I nodded. "I understand, madam."

"I believe that I am once again with child. I pray that it is so. But it is still too soon to be certain."

I must have looked startled, for Queen Elizabeth smiled. "I am thirty-five," she said, "not yet past my childbearing years. The king is but ten years older. We are both in good health. It would be a great blessing if I were to bear another son, for if something were to happen to Henry—" Her voice broke, and she stopped there, but I could complete her thought: . . . *there would be no male Tudor to inherit the throne.*

My hand rested on the stone sill of the window, and the queen laid her hand over mine and laced our fingers. Thus we stood, watching the young giant in the courtyard below us. He may have felt that he was being observed, for he paused and looked up at his mother's window. He smiled when he saw the queen, and when he noticed me by her side, he smiled even more broadly and bowed low.

How nice it would be, I thought, remembering the hours Henry and I spent together at the wedding, *if the duke and I could become friends.*

"As long as you are with us, my lady princess," the queen said, "you are under my special protection. It will not be easy, for the king can be quite difficult. I will do all I can for you, for he does sometimes listen to me. Do you understand, Lady Catherine?"

"I do, madam. And I am most grateful to you."

Later, when I had left the queen's apartments, I felt

more at ease than I had since Arthur's death. *All will be well,* I thought.

The days grew warm, though not so hot as a summer in Spain, and frequent rain showers kept Durham's gardens green and fragrant. In fair weather I strolled in those gardens, often sitting on a bench by the riverside and watching with my ladies as whole navies of majestic white swans drifted upstream or down, depending upon the tides. But, unless bidden by the queen, I seldom left the palace. I received no invitations from other English families, for I was officially in deep mourning, and I received few visitors.

Arthur's sisters, Princess Mary and Princess Margaret, were sometimes sent by their mother to call upon me. On several occasions the princesses were joined by their brother Henry, who never failed to amuse us with his wit and good humor and never left without teaching me another phrase or two of French. On one visit Henry and his sisters brought me the gift of a lively little black-and-white spaniel puppy.

"What shall you name him?" asked Henry, whose antics entertained me as much as the puppy's.

"Payaso," I answered, laughing. "The Spanish word for clown."

Henry clapped his hands delightedly. "Excellent!" he cried. "I shall tutor you in French, and you shall tutor me in Spanish!"

Soon after Henry's eleventh birthday on the twenty-eighth of June, his family invited me to join them on the royal barge as they traveled upstream for a picnic. I was very pleased to be included. But as I mused aloud about what a pleasant outing it would be, Doña Elvira interrupted me. "You are to decline, Catalina," she said.

"Decline?" I cried. "But why?"

"You are still in mourning," she pointed out. "For you to be seen enjoying yourself publicly only months after the death of your husband would be most unseemly. It will damage your reputation, which is my responsibility to protect, as I promised your excellent parents. I cannot permit it."

The crushing disappointment I felt gave way to resentment. I wanted to shout, *Does that mean I am to live in a convent?* But I swallowed both disappointment and resentment and instead employed reason. "The invitation has come from the queen herself," I said, keeping my voice calm, though I felt anything but. "To refuse her would be an insult to her and to the royal family."

At last my duenna relented, on the condition that she accompany me.

What a lovely day it turned out to be! The weather was sunny and bright and the royal party in a merry frame of mind as we boarded the beautiful barge. The queen seemed happy to see me, and the two princesses were in merry moods. Henry charmed us all—even the dour Doña Elvira—by singing and playing upon the lute as we drifted languorously among the great white swans. The oarsmen rowed us as far as Richmond, where a splendid feast had been laid out beneath the great oaks. When the tide turned, we boarded the barge once again for the return trip. I hated to see the day come to an end but comforted myself that more such lovely occasions would surely follow.

I particularly wished that I could see more of the delightful young duke. But as the summer of 1502 dragged on, I saw little of the royal family and nothing at all of Henry. I was grateful for the distraction the puppy offered, for my life was otherwise empty and dull. On one of her infrequent visits, I told Princess Margaret that I wished Henry might come again to see how much Payaso had grown.

"I am certain that he would enjoy that, but he cannot. Father has become so fearful of Henry's health and safety that he keeps him shut up with his tutors and forbids him to venture beyond the palace walls. He refuses to send Henry to Ludlow, fearing the air on the Marches may be unwholesome—perhaps that is what took Arthur's life. No one is allowed to speak to Henry except by permission of the king. Father has complete control over him. The only way my brother can leave his chambers is by passing through the king's."

"Henry is like a prisoner, then," I ventured.

"Yes, and he hates it so!" Margaret said.

His life is nearly as sequestered as mine, I thought. But

Henry was heir to the throne, and one day he would be free of his father's control. I wondered if I would ever free myself of Doña Elvira's.

Five months had passed since Arthur's untimely death, and I still had no idea what my future held. In that time I had received only two letters from my mother: the first offering condolences for my bereavement, the second advising me that their ambassadors would negotiate with King Henry for my future.

Following my wedding and departure for Ludlow, the witty and elegant Don Pedro de Ayala had been recalled to Spain by my parents, leaving his great rival, Don Rodrigo Gonzales de Puebla, as Spain's only ambassador to England. Soon after my arrival in London after Arthur's death, Don Rodrigo had come to call upon me. Into my privy chamber shambled a small, dark, and decidedly ill-favored man displaying none of Ayala's wit or polish.

In our first interview Don Rodrigo explained that in May, as soon as my parents learned of my widowhood, they had dispatched their special envoy, the duke of Estrada, to England with these instructions: Don Rodrigo was to call upon King Henry, demand the return of the 100,000 escudos that had been paid for my dowry, require immediate payment of the revenues due me as Arthur's widow, and insist that I be allowed to return to Spain at once. "And I have done as ordered, my lady."

I leaned forward eagerly. "With what result, Don Rodrigo?"

"The king assured me that he will think upon it. But there is more that you should know. The duke of Estrada received a second, secret, set of instructions from your parents. As soon as Henry, duke of York, is proclaimed prince of Wales, Estrada is to propose to the king that you marry the new prince."

Marry Henry? My head reeled with this news. "But Henry is only eleven years of age!" I stammered. "And I am nearly seventeen! It will be years before he is old enough to marry."

"Patience will be required, my lady," said Don Rodrigo. "It is a diplomatic ploy. King Henry will be forced to make a decision: to return you *and* your dowry to Spain, or to keep the dowry and marry you to his second son. Naturally, their majesties, the kings of Spain, hope that he will choose the marriage."

I had no say in this matter and expected none. If I could have had my wishes, I would have been on the next ship bound for Spain with never a backward glance. But marry Henry? I thought of him in the courtyard beneath his mother's window. Henry was a child! A great husky boy, but far from being a man.

Yet, even if King Henry accepted this proposal, the marriage would not be a simple matter, as Don Rodrigo then explained.

"Life can become very complicated at times, can it

not?" said Don Rodrigo with a sigh. "I speak to you now as one who has been trained in church law, and I will speak frankly, as I know your parents would wish. In the eyes of the church, you and Prince Arthur were married with all due ceremony. I and many others were witnesses to that. What only God has witnessed, however, is the consummation of that marriage—if indeed it was consummated?"

Don Rodrigo peered at me from beneath wild black brows arched like drawn bows. My face burning, I lowered my eyes and studied the tips of my ten fingers. I was unable to speak to him openly as I had to the queen.

The question hung unanswered. After a silence he continued unhurriedly, "If you were to be carrying Arthur's child, and if that child were to be a son, that is another matter. King Henry has refused to declare young Henry the new prince of Wales until he is absolutely certain that you will not provide an heir."

"I am not carrying a child," I replied. I had been asked that question by so many that, though it distressed me, I was able to answer forthrightly.

"Ah," said Don Rodrigo, stroking his greasy beard. "Then let me explain further: There is a biblical injunction that prohibits a man from marrying his brother's widow. A papal dispensation would have to be obtained in order for you to marry the duke of York."

I raised my eyes to meet his jet-black ones. "When

my sister Isabel died, her widower married my other sister, Maria. Is it not a similar thing?" I asked.

Don Rodrigo smiled, exposing long, yellow teeth. "Very similar. And in either case, it is the pope's decision in the matter." He squinted narrowly at me. "Pardon my seeming indelicacy, my lady princess, but these are important matters that will determine your future. Doña Elvira insists that your union was unconsummated. But Padre Alessandro insists that you and Prince Arthur lived as man and wife and that your husband sought your bed on numerous occasions. Whom am I to believe? Only you know the truth of the matter, my lady."

"Padre Alessandro said that?" I stared at Don Rodrigo in dismay, my face flushed with shame. Gathering my skirts, I fled weeping from the chamber while the ambassador stammered apologies. In my flight I nearly collided with Doña Elvira.

"What is it, Catalina?" she cried. She half carried, half dragged me to a private alcove. "Now tell me!" she commanded, gripping my hands tightly.

Still sobbing, I repeated the questions Don Rodrigo had put to me. "He claims to have heard these things from Padre Alessandro, and he has already written to warn my parents that a marriage with the duke of York might require the pope to intervene. Doña Elvira, how could my confessor have said such things? Surely Padre Alessandro knows the truth of the matter, as do you! I am still a virgin!"

"*¡Ese embustero!*" snarled Doña Elvira, her rage building. "That liar! Padre Alessandro is not fit to hear the confessions of a maiden as pure as she was on the day of her birth into this sinful world! And as for that boot-licking ambassador, I have always despised Rodrigo Gonzales de Puebla." *Un grosero malcriado,* she called him—an ill-mannered churl.

My duenna led me to my chambers and left me in the care of my ladies while she hurried off to berate Don Rodrigo and to demand his apology and his promise to write the truth of the matter to my parents.

Weeks later, after the ambassador had offered more apologies and sent off the letter, I received a brief note from my mother. "You have been ill served by Padre Alessandro, and he is being ordered to return at once to Spain."

Though I was angry that the priest had made false claims, I was also desolate. Padre Alessandro had been my tutor when I was a young girl, and he had been my chaplain since my arrival in England. But why had my confessor, whom I trusted, twisted my words and found meaning in them that I had not intended—and then passed on this so-called information to others?

On the occasion of my last meeting with Padre Alessandro, we both wept. "I meant only to help you, Catalina," he explained in a breaking voice. "By making clear that you were Arthur's wife in more than name only, I sought to prove you deserving of the honor due

his widow as well as the revenues to which you are en-
titled. Instead, it appears that I have done you harm."

That same day the priest was gone. I was left with
the detestable ambassador, Don Rodrigo; and Doña
Elvira, who now watched over me more fiercely than
ever.

CHAPTER 9

Another Death, Another Betrothal

Eltham Palace, September 1502

There had been times when Henry envied his older brother, who was always the center of attention. There had been times when Henry longed to be in Arthur's place but had to be content with being a duke. Second place scarcely counted.

Now Arthur was dead, and the world had changed. Suddenly everyone—especially his father—was watching him, hovering over Henry in ways he found oppressive. Why could they not simply leave him alone? Especially his father!

"Because, my lord," Brandon reminded him, "everything possible must be done to assure the well-being of England's future king."

"Then why has my father not proclaimed me prince of Wales?" Henry asked. "Arthur has been dead for five months now." He picked up a stone and hurled it as far as he could. Brandon picked up a stone and hurled it even farther.

"The king believes it possible that your sister-in-law is carrying Arthur's child," Brandon explained. "That child would then become your brother's heir, not you."

"But I have heard that she is not," Henry argued.

"In these matters, one must be absolutely certain. The king believes that he must wait until your brother has been dead for ten months."

"Ten? I thought it was nine."

"To be sure, my lord."

And so they waited. Henry had always been restive, and waiting made him peevish.

Then came the startling revelation that Henry's mother, the queen, was herself carrying a child. In September, when it was announced that the infant had quickened in the queen's womb, the king ordered Te Deums to be sung in joyous thanksgiving in churches throughout England. Everyone prayed that the child would be a son.

While others rejoiced, Henry's older sister, Margaret, worried. "Our mother is too old to safely bear another child," she told Henry. That frightened him, for he adored his mother as much as he feared his father.

There was yet another revelation.

The king had taken Henry for a day of hunting in Buckingham's deer park. They had spoken little until they rode toward the lodge at sunset. Without prelude the king said, "You may soon become betrothed to the princess of

Wales. The king and queen of Spain have informed me that they expect their widowed daughter to be betrothed to the heir to the English throne as soon as possible. I have not yet decided."

Betrothed to Catherine? *Lately Henry had heard rumors—mostly from Brandon—that the king was considering any number of European princesses with whose families he wished to contract a useful alliance. The possibility of marrying his widowed sister-in-law had never been mentioned, but now that his father had put forth the plan, Henry decided that he liked it. The princess was certainly well favored, with a fine complexion and that wonderful mass of shining auburn hair that hung nearly to her waist. Besides, she seemed so intelligent—unlike the simpering, empty-headed ladies in his mother's court. Not that his father had asked his opinion.*

He wondered what Arthur would think of his younger brother marrying his wife, besting him yet again.

Henry inclined his head. "As you wish, my lord."

The hunting party had reached the lodge, and nothing more was said. Later, though, Henry asked Brandon what he thought of the matter.

"My guess," *Brandon ventured,* "is that the king will betroth you to Princess Catherine. Otherwise, he might find that he has to return her and her dowry to Spain."

Whatever his father decided, Henry hoped the princess would remain in England. Whether they wed or not, he wanted Catherine as his friend. That, he was certain, would have pleased Arthur as much as it pleased him.

THE PLEASANT EARLY DAYS OF AUTUMN 1502 GAVE WAY to blustering chill and dampness. My life was as bleakly gray as the weather. I was invited nowhere and saw no one but Doña Elvira and the members of my little Spanish court. King Henry seemed to have forgotten me, though the queen occasionally sent me small gifts—a book she thought I might enjoy, a collar for Payaso. Don Rodrigo informed me that the negotiations for my marriage to young Henry remained stalled over issues of my dowry.

My health worsened. One day, as I lay suffering from a derangement of the stomach, my page announced the arrival of an envoy from my parents, the duke of Estrada. The duke was from one of Spain's oldest noble families, known to be loyal and trustworthy, but puffed up with self-importance and pompous in the extreme. I was forced to rouse myself from my bed to receive him.

Stroking his luxuriant mustaches, the duke delivered a long speech, choked with flowery phrases, informing me that my father had ordered him to prepare a ship to carry me and my retinue back to Spain.

"The ship already lies at anchor in the River Thames, my esteemed princess. Their Catholic majesties desire that you and the members of your court begin packing."

"Is it true?" I cried, my physical discomfort suddenly disappearing. "Swear to me that it is true!"

"Alas, no, my lady, it is not true," the duke confessed, his mustaches drooping forlornly. "But it must *appear* to be true."

My eyes filled with tears of disappointment. "Please explain this," I said miserably. "And, I beg you, do not disappoint me like this again."

"It is meant as a threat, my lady. King Ferdinand has not paid the second portion of your dowry since Arthur's death. If King Henry expects to collect that second portion and keep the first, then he must agree to a betrothal between you and his second son."

Now I understood that the sight of a ship lying ready to take me back to Spain was intended to force King Henry's hand. I had been in England long enough to know that the king would not willingly let 200,000 escudos escape from his treasury. And so, having no choice but to go through the pretense, I ordered my wooden chests to be brought from storage and a few items placed in them. Apparently the ploy was successful. Within days King Henry sent word that negotiations would begin on a new marriage contract. I quietly unpacked again, and the waiting ship disappeared from the Thames.

I consoled myself with the knowledge that, even if I had been allowed to return to Spain, it would have been for only a short time until my parents dispatched me to a new marriage. Perhaps, I thought, a future marriage to Henry could work out very well. I liked him. I believed we would be friends.

But still no money arrived for my household. Since Arthur's death my father had not sent any money for my expenses, and I had nothing with which to pay my servants or to support the members of my court. I learned from Don Rodrigo that Spain's engagement in a war in Italy had drained the royal treasury and that even he had not received his ambassador's salary in over a year.

Surely, I thought, my father would not allow me to live in penury. My ladies and I repaired our threadbare gowns as best we could, though there were few reasons to do so. I was not invited to any events at court—in part because I was still officially in mourning. My duenna believed it her duty to keep me in seclusion. My seventeenth birthday was a poor affair, for there was no money to order a banquet. My minstrels played and Santiago and Urraca performed new tricks, but nothing cheered me. With a heavy heart I remembered the previous year when I was Arthur's bride and every imaginable dish had been presented at our banquet table at Bewdley.

Yuletide also found little celebration at Durham. On the twenty-sixth of December, the feast of Saint Stephen, Arthur's sisters, Mary and Margaret, along with Henry, came to deliver Yuletide greetings. I had looked forward to their visit and had a small token for each of them: embroidered ribbons to mark the place in their missals. But their talk was all about the Yuletide merrymaking they had enjoyed at Richmond, the great feast that had taken place in observance of Margaret's thirteenth birthday, and the plans being made for Twelfth Night. I had no part in any of it. In the end their visit left me feeling more disconsolate than ever.

There was another reason for my gloom: Henry was now a half year short of his twelfth birthday. Because a betrothal seemed likely, I did hope that we could become better acquainted. But Doña Elvira refused to allow it, insisting that we must not spend time together at all, even in the company of his sisters and all of my ladies. "I permitted it at Dogmersfield. I shall not permit it again. We cannot allow even a hint of impropriety to besmirch your spotless reputation."

One day we received word that the young Tudors were on their way to Durham. When Doña Elvira saw that I meant to defy her and welcome them, she took the precaution of locking me in my chamber and sent word that I was unable to receive visitors. Francesca found a key and unlocked the door, but it was too late. The Tudors had gone. I was so distressed and angry that I refused to speak to my duenna for more than a week.

My anger deepened at Doña Elvira's ironfisted rule, but I believed I had no way to loosen her grip without help. Everyone feared her. All I could do, for now, was to observe this boy, with his increasing good looks and high spirits, and to steal glances at him out of the corner of my eye whenever we happened to be at mass or some large public occasion. And I wondered what he might be thinking about me.

In January the court moved to the Tower of London, and there, on the second of February, Queen Elizabeth was delivered of her eighth child—not the hoped-for son, but another daughter. Nine days later, on her thirty-sixth birthday, the queen was dead of childbed fever. Her infant daughter, christened Catherine in honor of the queen's sister, lived only a few days more. Once again the royal family was plunged into deepest sorrow, and I with them, for I had lost my protector and friend.

The death watch over the queen's body had not yet ended when King Henry summoned me to his chambers. I knelt three times as I approached him, and when the king raised me up I saw that he had become an old man. It was as though he had shrunken to a poor copy of the vigorous man I had first met at Dogmersfield only sixteen months earlier. His shrewd eyes swept over me, as they had at that first meeting, but now they seemed haunted, nearly lifeless.

He wasted no time with an exchange of polite phrases. "Ten months have passed since the death of Prince Arthur. Is it true then, madam, as you claim, that you are not carrying Arthur's child, and that you will not provide the kingdom with his heir?"

"What you say is true, my lord," I answered.

He made no reply, merely sighing deeply and dismissing me with a wave of his bony hand before he turned away.

A few days later on the eighteenth of February, 1503, I attended a grimly formal ceremony in which Henry, duke of York, was created prince of Wales. Befitting the occasion Henry was more serious and subdued than I had ever seen him. Only once in the course of the long ritual did he glance in my direction, but I was heavily veiled in black, and he could not read the message my eyes held for him: *I shall be your friend.*

Scarcely a month after that somber occasion, Maria de Salinas flew into my chambers with the latest court rumor. Maria was being courted by the duke of Derby, a grandson of the king's stepfather, and so was privy to much gossip. "Catalina, imagine this," she whispered excitedly. "King Henry is in search of a new wife!"

I was mending some table linens that had fallen into disrepair. "So soon?" I bit off the end of a thread. "The good queen has been dead for little more than a month."

"The king believes that he must tend to this matter immediately. He fears that some disaster might befall the new prince of Wales, as it did Arthur, and he will be left with only daughters. A new wife might produce yet another son for him."

I was not much surprised that King Henry wished to marry. I understood his concerns, for the death of my brother had left my parents without a male heir. But I gave no further thought to the king's predicament until the duke of Estrada strutted into my chambers puffed and preening with his own importance.

"What now, good sir," I gibed, "another order to begin imaginary packing for yet another phantom ship?"

But the duke saw no humor in my little jest and began one of his lengthy speeches. At last he reached his point: "King Henry the Seventh has informed me that he wishes to marry you, my lady princess."

I was shocked speechless. A look of horror must have crossed my face. I could not imagine myself wed to a man thirty years older than I, his teeth already blackened, his eyes rheumy, his skin like old parchment. *I, marry King Henry?*

"Does my mother, the queen, know?" I asked in a voice quavering with distress when I was again able to speak.

"She knows, madam. And she has refused to entertain his suit. The queen has said she would rather return you to Spain than allow such a marriage."

I nearly fainted with relief.

But it was the ambassador, Don Rodrigo, who supplied the practical details that the more refined duke had omitted: "The marriage would not be useful to Spain. Your sons would be in line for the throne after the new prince of Wales. You would have little power or influence over either the present or the future king. That power and influence is naturally what your parents require of your marriage."

I sat with bowed head, listening to his blunt but honest words. Whatever my mother's reasons, I was deeply grateful.

In April I observed the first anniversary of my husband's death. I was more than ready to throw off the mourning garments I had worn for a year and to seek some mild diversions in the life of the English court. Though Doña Elvira continued to cling to me like a shadow and to rule my days with an unbending will, there was no point in confronting her. With so little money in the household coffers, there was nothing at all to spend on pleasure anyway. The Great Feast of Easter was scarcely different from any other meal at my table—a little bread, a little meat, some poor wine.

When Juan de Cuero, my treasurer, refused to permit me to sell two or three pieces of plate in order to feed my household and to meet my obligations to my servants, I wrote to my parents yet again, pleading with them. My father answered that letter swiftly with a firm negative: The plate had to be preserved as part of my dowry and could not be touched.

But what, please God, was I to do in the meantime?

————

At last, on the twenty-third of June, five days before Henry's twelfth birthday, a marriage treaty was signed, betrothing me to the new prince of Wales. Certain agreements had been reached: The dowry—always the dowry!—would remain unchanged; the wedding would take place when Henry reached the age of fifteen, providing the pope granted the proper dispensations, and providing the balance of my dowry had been paid over to King Henry—100,000 escudos, part in gold coin and part in jewels and plate.

The day after the marriage treaty was signed, Henry and I celebrated our betrothal with a great banquet. This was the first occasion of rejoicing and merriment since weeks before Arthur's death. I managed to put one of my gowns in good repair, sat between the king and his aged mother, and once again danced with my ladies, feeling almost lighthearted. My future husband led his sister, Princess Margaret, in a lively galliard with its rapid steps and vigorous leaps. *I must learn those steps,* I thought, watching as Henry danced with the abandon of a boy with no care in this world but to make merry.

The mourning period was over. I was betrothed to the future king of England. I would once more be invited to court and treated with the honor and respect that were due me. Surely my life would now improve.

Still, I was past seventeen, an age at which most young women were already married. Yet I would have to wait three long years until all the conditions of the betrothal were reached and I would once again be a wife. I felt that I was already growing old, my child-bearing years fleeting, while my future husband—his cheeks flushed with the exertions of the dance—had not yet reached manhood.

But I knew that waiting was called for. I had already begun to imagine the man—and the king—that Henry would become. And I would be his queen. I was prepared to wait as long as I must.

CHAPTER 10

Waiting

Richmond Palace, September 1503

The king informed Henry that the marriage would not take place for several years. "And much could happen in the meantime. There is not a monarch in all of Christendom who would not be pleased to wed his daughter to the next king of England. Betrothals are made to be broken."

Henry wished to ask questions. Were betrothals so easily broken? Was this not the same as breaking one's word? What would then become of the princess? Would she be sent back to Spain? What other princesses were being considered? But his father did not allow such questions, and they remained unasked.

More troublesome to Henry than the matter of a broken betrothal was his father's new attitude toward him.

Since Henry had been invested as prince of Wales and given a number of other titles, the king insisted upon keeping him constantly by his side wherever he went—to Richmond, Greenwich, or Westminster. Brandon and one or two others traveled with them.

"You have much to learn, my son," his father often reminded him. "I sometimes worry that I have not enough time in which to teach you."

Lessons in kingship were constant and ongoing, with his father's own history as the text. Again Henry heard the story of how his father had killed his rival, King Richard III, on Bosworth Field and since then had faced rebels, pretenders to the throne, and threats to his own life. "Seizing power is not difficult. It takes only courage," said his father. "Holding power—now that is the challenge. It takes shrewdness and ruthlessness. When threatened, do not hesitate. Strike fearlessly. Even if it means sending to the block men you have considered your friends."

King Henry reminded his son that he himself had only a few years earlier ordered the execution of the earl of Warwick, who had been heard to make claims to the throne.

"Do whatever you must to keep the crown on your own head," his father advised. "The end justifies the means."

King Henry also had a great deal to say about other European monarchs. The French, warned King Henry, were never to be trusted in an alliance. Maximilian, the Holy Roman Emperor, was a force to be reckoned with. His son, Philip, was married to Catherine's sister, Juana, *and their children would one day inherit all of Maximilian's titles, plus the crowns of Spain. But Maximilian was fickle in his loyalties and might turn at any time. It was impossible to count on the emperor.*

"And that damnable Ferdinand and Isabella! Spending every piece of gold in the Spanish treasury to pursue their war in Italy. And to what end? They are unable to pay the money due on their daughter's dowry, or even to support her and her court."

Henry listened carefully to his father's words and observed his actions. The prince had begun to imagine himself in his father's place, as king of England, all-powerful, beloved by the common people, and, if necessary, feared by noblemen with a hunger for power. At first he had enjoyed the new role of cherished son and the attentions now lavished upon him. But now he chafed under his father's stern restrictions and dreaded the outbursts of temper that had become more and more frequent.

Only Brandon's company gave him any relief from his father's demands and made the prince's life bearable.

Someday in the future I was to become the queen of England, yet my present life did not improve as I had every right to expect and, in fact, seemed more precarious than ever. I still had no money to support myself and my household.

Now that I was betrothed to Henry, the ambassador encouraged me to write to my father-in-law, explaining my impoverished circumstances. "Certainly the king knows of it," said Don Rodrigo. "But he is unlikely to offer aid unless you petition him for it." I followed Don Rodrigo's advice and sent the letter. The answer was immediate.

"You are like a daughter to me," King Henry replied fondly, apparently forgetting that not long before he had thought of me as a future wife. "You have only to inform me of your needs, and they shall be taken care of." He granted me an allowance of one hundred crowns a month from the royal treasury for the maintenance of my household.

It was a generous sum but still not enough to support a household of sixty. I would have to make do. I remembered gratefully how my mother had drilled my sisters and me in frugal household management, lessons we had scorned at the time.

Once the allowance had been settled, I was again

treated with the honor and dignity due a highborn princess, and my spirits lifted. I wrote happily to my sister, Juana, describing my new life: I attended court functions and traveled with my suite as the royal court moved from one palace to another. I accompanied the royal family on hunting trips and danced with my ladies at splendid banquets, even with our shabby gowns. Occasionally Prince Henry was present, but we were seldom given the opportunity to speak together, and I had to be contented with smiles and bows. I ignored Doña Elvira's disapproving frowns and clucks of the tongue.

In August Princess Margaret departed for Scotland to marry James IV, and she invited me to ride part of the way with her huge retinue. From Don Pedro de Ayala, the former ambassador to Scotland, I had heard so many stories of the wildness of the Scots and their complete lack of civility that I wept with her as she set out for the north.

But Princess Margaret had other reasons for her tears. "My dear mother spent her last remaining strength helping me to assemble my household goods," she confided as we rode together in her litter. She gazed out at the long line of wheeled carts creaking under the weight of her belongings. "Sometimes I blame myself for her death. Perhaps the effort weakened her."

This reminded me of my own dear mother and how deeply I missed her. Impulsively, I grasped Margaret's hand and brought it to my lips. "But, dear Margaret, we must go bravely to our future," I said, wiping away her tears and mine as well.

As the procession neared Hatfield, we made our last farewells, and I turned back toward London. For days afterward I felt lonelier for her going and far less brave than I wished.

When I first arrived in England I had hoped that Arthur's mother, Queen Elizabeth, would instruct me in the ways of the English court. I am certain that we would have drawn quite close had not so many tragedies intervened. With the good queen dead, the king's mother, Lady Margaret Beaufort, countess of Richmond and Derby, had taken over the management of the royal household, watching over both Henrys, father and son, as well as little Princess Mary.

Despite the ten-year difference in our ages, I had formed an easy friendship with Princess Mary. She came to visit often, bringing her lute, and I taught her to play some pretty songs. Though only eight years old, the princess was a keen observer of her family. She often spoke of her grandmother, who had rules for everything in the household.

"There are rules for what we eat, what we drink, what we put on. My lady grandmother has ordered Father to wear a red nightcap with a hole in the top for vapors to escape, in order to sweeten his breath. She has rules for how Father's bed must be made: Every morning the gentleman of the bedchamber orders a servant to leap up and down upon the king's bed to fluff up the mattresses. The linen sheets are laid on in a particular order, and certain herbs are tucked into the pillows—to keep away the fleas, you know—and then the coverlets are piled on, and at the end the priest is summoned to sprinkle holy water over it all. Now the same is true for Henry. He has always been her favorite—after Father, of course."

"And *your* bed?" I asked Mary.

The little princess giggled. "Only the holy water," she said. "But no one leaps up and down upon it, and I do wish they would!"

I knew that Lady Margaret had been married three times. Her first husband, Edmund Tudor, left her a widow a few months before her son, Henry, was born when she was just thirteen. She married again, this time to Henry Stafford, who soon died. Shortly after her third marriage, to a widower, Thomas Stanley, earl of Derby, she took a vow of chastity and ever since had lived a deeply pious life, abstaining from banquets and entertainments, dressing in simple kirtles and shunning elaborate gowns and jewels.

"Grandmother's prayers begin long before the sun rises," Mary said. "She hears mass five times a day, attends morning and evening prayers with her gentlewomen, and makes a confession every third day. She eats scarcely anything—no breakfast and only a little dinner—and she strictly observes every fast day. Beneath her kirtle she wears a girdle made of coarse hair that rubs against her skin until it bleeds."

Now that I was betrothed to Lady Margaret's only living grandson, I quickly learned that I was under her intense scrutiny. The old countess seemed to watch everything, to miss not the smallest detail. As the new year of 1504 began, she summoned me to visit her at Richmond.

I was determined not to appear uneasy about my interview, but as soon as I had been ushered into her chambers by an elderly page, I felt that she took in every inch of me and found me lacking, beginning with my threadbare gown. She would not have known that my father had sent me no money, unless the king told her. She may not have realized that I had only the hundred crowns the king allowed me each month. If she had known, she may not have realized that was not enough.

Lady Margaret began by greeting me in French. I recognized some of the phrases, but I could not think quickly enough to frame a suitable reply. I grasped for words that would not come and finally managed to stammer a response in Latin.

"You do not speak French, my dear princess?" the old countess asked in Latin, her eyebrows lifted. Her eyes were shrewd, I thought, like the king's.

"I do not, Lady Margaret," I whispered.

She shifted to English and was rewarded by my

gaping look of incomprehension. Her eyebrows plowed into a frown. "Nor English, either?"

"It has not been possible, my lady," I replied.

"Not possible?"

"I seldom hear English spoken, madam. All of my English staff resigned after Arthur's death. I have no one to teach me."

But the countess brushed aside my excuses. "You have been here for how long, Catherine? More than two years? And yet it seems that nothing of our very practical and, shall I say, *forceful* English language has made its way to your lips? True, English may seem to lack the elegance of French and the intellectual precision of Latin, but many of your new countrymen find it useful. Perhaps you, as their future queen, might find it useful as well."

"Yes, madam," I whispered, my head bowed in shame.

It seemed that the interview was at an end, and I fled, weak with humiliation.

In spring Princess Mary invited me to go hawking at Eltham with her and her cousins. Naturally, I wanted to accept. Every invitation was an opportunity for me to become more familiar with the ways of the English court, to learn a few words of their language, and perhaps to see Prince Henry. But it seemed the better I got along with the English, the more tightly my duenna gripped my reins in her clenched fist. Once again Doña Elvira refused permission, falling back upon her usual explanation of her duty to protect my reputation.

I had heard these same words dozens of times, and they infuriated me. "Must I live like this for two more years, until I am wed?" I cried. "I am no longer a child! I am a full-grown woman of eighteen. I have already had a husband! In what manner is this improper?"

She answered only with the haughty look I had learned to detest, a look that said, "If you must ask why it is improper, it simply shows that you are incapable of judging for yourself."

I seethed with resentment, yet I felt powerless in the face of her extraordinary will and, above all, my loyalty to my mother's wishes. Would my mother have issued the same edict? I no longer believed she would. After the hawking party had gone, I began to suffer attacks of ague. My complexion faded, my appetite declined, and a physician was summoned to bleed me. Every time I opened my eyes, there was Doña Elvira, and I shut my eyes again. *The next time I receive an invitation,* I thought, *I shall accept, no matter what my duenna says.* As soon as I had made that determination, I began to feel stronger.

Yet who else had I? Queen Elizabeth was dead. The old countess offered only criticism. As time wore on, King Henry paid me less and less attention. Perhaps because of this, the number of invitations from court declined, and those that arrived were to events of little interest or importance. I heard nothing from Prince Henry, and, in truth, I was not certain that I was much on his mind.

I found little comfort in my own household. My ladies were lonely and restless. Members of my small court bickered among themselves. Doña Elvira's son, Don Iñigo, insisted that he should have authority over my pages as well as over my mules, putting him at odds with Cuero's son. I tried to keep the peace.

My allowance from the king of one hundred crowns a month barely met the current expenses of my household and did not help to make up their back wages. There was never anything left over at the end of the month, and I was sinking ever deeper into debt. Despite my pleas, Cuero continued to refuse to allow me to sell a few pieces of my plate. And my parents sent no help, because they had nothing to send.

That left only Doña Elvira and Don Rodrigo Gonzales de Puebla, who could scarcely bear to be in one another's presence. "Mark my words, he is working for the interests of the English, not of the Spanish," Doña Elvira insisted. "The ambassador is in the pay of King Henry, who bribes him well," she continued. "Your father sends you no help because Don Rodrigo tells him nothing but honeyed lies to set his mind at ease; that all is well with you and your complaints can safely be ignored! Puebla eats at the king's table and seeks to advance himself at court with the most abject fawning and flattery. No doubt he lies to King Henry as well, and that is why the king treats you so coldly."

I hated to agree with her about anything, but I too, was beginning to mistrust the ambassador. It did not occur to me to mistrust Doña Elvira.

One pleasant summer afternoon, a smiling and blushing Maria de Salinas brought me her good news: Edward Stanley, the young gentleman who had been courting her, had asked for her hand in marriage.

"I do love him," she said, glowing with happiness.

Maria was sixteen. If she were back in Spain, she would certainly have been married by now. She had always expected to find a husband in England. Edward was certainly suitable. His grandfather was Thomas Stanley, earl of Derby, husband of the king's mother! Lady Margaret and the earl had given their approval, the king had given his, but there remained the matter of a dowry: Maria had none. It was my responsibility to provide it, and I had not a single escudo to give her. With the hope that my mother might send something, I wrote to her. We waited, but the months passed with no reply. With every passing day our hopes grew dimmer, and our hearts grew heavier.

As I approached my nineteenth birthday in the autumn of 1504, I had lived in England for three years. An entire twelvemonth had passed without papal approval for my marriage to the prince of Wales. The pope had died soon after the request for a dispensation was delivered to him, and a month later his successor was also dead. After the election of yet another pope, Julius II, the request passed into his hands. On his decision I now waited.

I wrote again to my mother, of this matter, as well as of Maria's dowry. Still there was no reply.

I began to worry. My mother had explained before I left that I must not count on letters, for it could take many weeks and even months, when weather prevented ships from sailing, for a letter to reach her and for a reply to make its way back to me. "There will be many people to help you in times of difficulty," she assured me. "And I have trained you well to find your own way. You must think on my words, and remember what I have taught you."

On the twenty-sixth of November, 1504, I posted a third, pleading letter to my mother on Maria's behalf. Surely she would reply to this request! A few weeks later Don Rodrigo shuffled into my apartments with a letter bearing the royal seal of Aragon. "I fear that I bring news of the worst sort, my lady," he mumbled as he handed over the letter.

My fingers trembled as I broke the seal and scanned the brief message from my father. My mother was dead. On the very day I had written my last letter to her, my mother lay dying. I was sobbing as I passed the letter to

Doña Elvira, who let out a shriek as though mortally wounded. Don Rodrigo offered his condolences and left quietly as my duenna and I wept, each of us wrapped in our separate grief.

I had known when I left Spain that I might never see my father and mother again, but I had pushed that understanding to the farthest corner of my mind. It was true that I had had few letters from her, as she had warned me. Yet I had always been comforted by the knowledge that somewhere, though far away, she cared about me deeply. Now she was gone forever, and my world seemed a cold and frightening place without her. Bereft, I plunged into a sea of grief.

I was joined in my grieving by Doña Elvira, whose loss seemed as deep as my own. In the first days of pain and sorrow, my duenna and I spent long hours together, speaking of my mother. "I loved Queen Isabella above all women," said Doña Elvira. "Her strength, her intelligence, her goodness. She has always been the heart and soul of Castilla. Without her, there is no Spain."

Much later I learned that, at the hour when Death came for my mother, he was raced to her bedside by a messenger bearing a letter from Pope Julius, granting the dispensation for my marriage. Believing my future was finally assured, my mother had died in peace. For that I was most grateful.

But there was no dowry for Maria.

CHAPTER 11

Treachery and Deceit

Richmond Palace, June 1505

Tomorrow, the twenty-eighth of June, would be Henry's fourteenth birthday. Plans had been made for a grand celebration of his coming of age: Henry would no longer be a boy. He already had the form and size of a man, taller than his father and nearly all the men in his father's court, though not yet as tall as Brandon. There would be feasting and music, but Henry looked forward most excitedly to the tournaments, in which he expected that he would perform splendidly. Princess Catherine would be seated among the spectators with her ladies, watching him and certain to be impressed.

The prince, with the help of Brandon, was trying on a suit of fine new armor recently completed for tomorrow's tournament. Just then, a page entered the armory and announced that the king would see the prince of Wales at once in the royal chambers.

Henry sighed. These summonses arrived from the king several times daily, and Henry had no choice but to obey. He expected this would have to do with the next day's ceremonies. Perhaps his father was bestowing upon him a few more titles, though Henry could not think which ones he had not yet received. Or perhaps some additional duty was about to be thrust upon him. Whatever it was, Henry was eager to be done with it. Brandon helped him out of the clumsy armor, and Henry followed the page to his father's chambers.

King Henry sat at a table, writing on a sheet of parchment. Henry knelt and waited until his father laid aside his quill and gazed at him. "Tomorrow is the day upon which you reach the formal age of consent," said the king. "Therefore, you have serious business that must be taken care of today."

Henry bowed his head. "Yes, my lord."

"You will appear before the bishop of Winchester and renounce your betrothal to Princess Catherine."

Henry's head jerked upright. His father had warned him of the possibility, but he was nevertheless surprised. "Renounce my betrothal? On what grounds, my lord?"

"That you were a minor at the time the betrothal was contracted," snapped the king. "As of today you are still a minor, and hence the marriage contract is legally null *and void." The king folded his hands and smiled with satisfaction.*

"But what of Princess Catherine?" Henry asked the question he had not asked before. "What will become of her?"

The king laughed, a harsh, bitter sound. "That is a question her father should have been asking all along. The king of Spain has not kept his side of the bargain. Where is the gold that he promised to pay me as her dowry?" The king leaned closer to the prince, his eyes glinting. "Think of this, Henry: Once the betrothal has been broken off, you are free! We can find you a far more suitable wife, one who is much, much richer. There is doubtless a far better bargain to be had than your wretched little Spanish princess in her tattered gowns."

Henry stared at his father, his mind in turmoil. He was beginning to understand the extent of the king's greed. His father was already the richest man in the kingdom. Why then was he driven to seek even greater wealth? Henry thought of Catherine. He pitied her, and he also liked her. But beyond mere liking, there was something more, something deeper: He had come to believe that marrying her was a debt of honor he owed his dead brother. He was about to say this to his father when a trumpet announced the arrival of members of the king's privy council.

The king dismissed Henry before he could utter a word. "Be ready to meet with the bishop within the hour. Speak of this to no one."

FOR WEEKS PRINCESS MARY HAD EXCITEDLY DESCRIBED to me the festivities planned for Prince Henry's fourteenth birthday. There would be banquets with music and dancing and disguisings, followed by tournaments in which the prince was expected to demonstrate his prowess in the tiltyard. The more she told me, the more eagerly I looked forward to what would surely be a splendid event.

Again I appealed to my treasurer, Juan de Cuero. "As Prince Henry's betrothed wife, I shall be among the most honored ladies at the birthday celebration. It would be unseemly for me to appear in one of my worn-out gowns." I produced a gold bracelet set with jewels. "Sell this, I beg you, that I may present myself to the royal family decently dressed."

"My lady princess, I cannot," said Cuero, sadly shaking his head. "The bracelet belongs to your dowry."

I implored him. He was adamant. I wept. He appeared to weaken. I fell to my knees and begged. At last he agreed. The bracelet was sold, and I ordered a new gown, to be prepared in all haste, in time for the celebration on the twenty-eighth of June.

But days passed, and no invitation arrived. Had it somehow gone astray? I questioned my servants, who swore no message had been delivered. Time was growing short. Perhaps, I thought, King Henry had decided to hold the festivities at Greenwich or one of the other royal palaces, and Doña Elvira had taken it upon herself to refuse me permission to attend.

"What do you know of this, Doña Elvira?" I asked suspiciously.

"Nothing whatsoever," she replied haughtily. "Perhaps your questions are better directed to our ambassador. It is Don Rodrigo who knows the king's mind, not I."

The night before the banquet, as I lay sleepless and miserable in my bed, I finally admitted to myself that I had not been invited after all. But why? Surely Henry would have wanted me, his betrothed, to be present. Was it the king, then? Had something happened of which I had no knowledge? Where *was* that perfidious ambassador, Don Rodrigo? Early the next morning, exhausted after my sleepless night and torn between outrage and bitter disappointment, I ordered my beautiful new gown packed away.

On the afternoon of the banquet I sat in the garden by the river with my ladies, my spirits at their lowest ebb, and watched listlessly as Payaso romped about, dashing to the river's edge to bark at the swans. Inez and Francesca gathered nosegays of roses, while Maria sat quietly by my side, mending one of my petticoats. We were always mending something! Suddenly clouds gathered and darkened, blocking the sun. I called for Payaso, and we rushed to the palace as the first cold drops of rain began to fall.

Just as we reached cover, Rodrigo Gonzales de Puebla was announced. I invited the ambassador to my privy chamber, observing as I did so that his garments were in even worse condition than my own, patches upon patches, stains upon stains. My ladies immediately vanished—they liked the ambassador no more than I did—but Doña Elvira appeared, making it plain that she had no intention of leaving me alone with him. For once I welcomed her presence.

Don Rodrigo paced agitatedly the length and breadth of my chamber. Finally he halted before me and blurted out his stunning news: "Prince Henry has broken off your betrothal."

"Broken it off?" My chest tightened so that I could scarcely breathe, and I sank weakly onto a bench.

"It pains me to tell you this, my lady princess. Yesterday Prince Henry appeared in secret before the bishop of Winchester and repudiated the marriage contract. The prince claimed it was made before he reached the age of consent."

"What stupid tales you carry!" interrupted Doña Elvira, glaring at the ambassador.

"Unfortunately, my tales are wholly true, madam," Don Rodrigo replied with a perfunctory bow in her direction. "There are no secrets that cannot be found out."

I covered my face with my hands. Never in my life had I felt so ill-used, or so frightened of what my future now held.

"I have more to tell," the ambassador said, his voice cracking.

I dropped my hands and gazed up at him tearfully. "Then tell it, Don Rodrigo," I said. "Tell all of it now and be done."

The ambassador sighed and rubbed his nose, another of his irritating habits. "King Henry has informed me that he is no longer obligated to continue your allowance of one hundred crowns per month."

"And he intends to reduce it to—?" I asked, my mouth dry as dust.

"To nothing, my lady."

I could not find the words to reply to this abysmal news, but Doña Elvira attacked the ambassador with every insult at her command. "*¡Cobarde!*" she cried. "Coward! Did you leave your manhood in Spain? Why have you permitted this to happen?"

Don Rodrigo recoiled before her sharp-tongued assault. "Doña Elvira, please understand that I can do nothing. When I protested the cruelty of his decision, King Henry merely referred me to King Ferdinand. 'He is her father, let him support her.' Those were his words." Puebla turned to me, but I could scarcely bring myself to look at him. "Before I came here today, I dispatched a courier with a letter to your father. He must be made to understand how desperate your situation has become. For my part, my lady, I would gladly help you if I could, but as you can see, I have nothing of my own. My purse is empty."

Doña Elvira hurled a few more epithets at the cringing ambassador. As soon as he had fled my chambers, I slipped into the darkest despair for the hopelessness of my life. I had once envisioned the brightest of futures, and now it seemed I had no future at all.

I was not the only one who had lost hope. Maria de Salinas also saw her dreams shattered. When it became apparent that she would have no dowry, negotiations for Maria's betrothal to Edward Stanley were called off. Her eyes were still red and swollen from weeping for the loss of her true love when Doña Elvira's son, Don Iñigo, began to court her.

I had suspected for some time that my equerry fancied himself in love with the charming Maria, admired by all for her beauty. But Don Iñigo was of a dour temperament—much like Doña Elvira's—and his person not at all engaging. Beyond his hearing, and his mother's, we called him *El Sapo*: "The Toad."

"Never, never, never!" Maria cried out as she wept in my arms. "Better to drown myself in the River Thames than to accept *El Sapo* as a husband!"

When Doña Elvira learned of Maria's refusal of Don Iñigo, she reacted with disgust. "I have always considered Maria rather stupid," she snorted contemptuously. "Now I am certain of it. My son would make her a fine and loyal husband, and he will take her without a dowry. Who else is willing to do that?"

I knew that Doña Elvira was right. Without a dowry, Maria had little chance of marriage. But I also knew that once Maria's mind was made up, she was unlikely to change it. I tried to keep my friend and my duenna apart until Maria was of a calmer mind, but one dreadful day their mutual animosity erupted.

"I frankly cannot imagine why my son would want to marry a person as obdurate and ill-bred as you, Maria!" said Doña Elvira.

"Because, Doña Elvira, he is as vain and selfish as his mother, and he does not take into account the feelings of anyone but himself!" cried Maria.

I intervened between the two and later begged Maria to reconsider. "Maria," I pleaded with her, "until my father sends the dowry he owes and everything is made right and I am actually married to Prince Henry, I shall not be able to help you. I beg you to understand that!"

"But you will never marry Prince Henry, Lady Catalina. Do you not understand *that*?" Aghast at her intemperate words, she turned and fled sobbing from the chamber.

Rarely had I lost my temper with Maria, my oldest and closest friend. I regret to say that on that day, I did.

"I *will* marry him!" I shouted after her. "How dare you speak otherwise? I believed you were loyal to me, but I see that you are not!"

The door slammed, and I thought I was alone. I was shocked then when Francesca stepped out of an alcove at the far end of the chamber, holding a stocking that she had been mending. I realized that she had been there all along, a witness to this unpleasant scene.

She stared at me for a moment and then said quietly, "Maria dares speak the truth to you, Catalina, if no one else will. It is not she who is disloyal to you. For once, my lady, remove the blindfold from your eyes and look about you!"

Her harsh words stunned me. *Who would be disloyal to me?* The very idea wounded me deeply. I seized Francesca's shoulders and gazed into her eyes. "Tell me, Francesca."

She opened her mouth as if to speak and then closed it again and shook her head. "Forgive me, my lady, but I cannot."

"Francesca, tell me!" I cried. "I demand that you tell me!"

Suddenly the door burst open, and Doña Elvira swept in. "Tell her what, Francesca?"

Francesca recoiled, pale with fright. "Tell her—Tell her whom I love," she stammered. She dropped me a low curtsy and rushed away.

Hurt, angry, and confused, I resolved that I would

somehow determine the truth for myself. I soon concluded that I knew the answer: Don Rodrigo. It should have been clear to me all along why my life had sunk to such a low state: Why my father had sent no money, and why the king no longer provided my allowance. I had disliked the unpleasant little ambassador from the first, but now my distrust of him was total.

The more I thought of the matter, the more convinced I became. And Doña Elvira never missed an opportunity to feed my suspicion.

"Do you still believe that treacherous Puebla supports you and your rightful claims as a princess of Spain?" she asked spitefully. "He does not!"

"But what am I to do?" I implored. "Please advise me, Doña Elvira."

Doña Elvira deliberated for a moment. "I have a suggestion, Catalina: Write to your sister, Juana, and appeal to her. Ask her to meet with you. Now that she is queen of Castilla, surely she and her husband will come to your aid."

At once my spirits brightened. After my mother's death, Spain had broken again into the two parts, Castilla and Aragon, that had been united long ago by my parents' marriage. My father still wore the crown of Aragon, but Juana had inherited the throne of Castilla from our mother. Though she lived in Flanders with her husband, Philip, she was bound to fill Queen Isabella's place. She had the means to help me. At Doña Elvira's urging, I wrote to Juana, suggesting a meeting, and dispatched the letter at once.

Sooner than I dared wish for, I had a reply from my sister. Juana expressed pleasure at the idea of seeing me again and urged me to propose that King Henry and the royal family cross the Channel to Calais. I would naturally be invited to accompany them, and Juana and Philip would meet us there. How festive it would be! How splendid!

In a joyful mood I wrote another letter, this one to King Henry, describing the plan. I went off in search of a messenger to carry my letter and my sister's to the king.

As the messenger left Durham House on horseback, bound for Richmond, I happened to encounter the treacherous ambassador, Don Rodrigo. So high had my confidence risen that I thoughtlessly told him of my plan to see my sister and Philip.

Don Rodrigo blanched, and a look of dismay crossed his face. I saw at once that something was wrong. This chance meeting was surely a bad omen. Perhaps I had interfered in one of his little plots! Well, that was unfortunate for him!

"Good day, sir," I said and walked rapidly away, leaving him standing with his mouth agape.

I had barely reached the door of my chambers when Don Rodrigo caught up to me, seized my hand, and dropped to his knees, white as death, sweat beading his broad forehead. "Madam," he cried, tears streaming down his face and his voice thick with emotion, "I beg you, listen to me. I speak only the truth, I swear it, and you must pay heed. Your future and the future of Spain depend upon it."

Angrily I snatched my hand from his and was about to walk away again when I changed my mind and decided to hear him out.

"Speak, then," I said icily, my arms folded across my chest. I saw that he was trembling.

"My lady princess, without your knowledge you have been caught up in an intrigue against your father. At the center of it is Doña Elvira."

Doña Elvira? At the center of an intrigue? Impossible!

I knew that Doña Elvira's brother, Don Juan Manuel, was my father's ambassador to the court of Emperor Maximilian, Philip's father. Don Juan had been loyal to my mother as long as she lived, but I now learned from the ambassador that Don Juan hated my father. "Don Juan leads a group of discontented Spanish noblemen determined to end your father's rule in Castilla through your sister," explained Puebla, his voice hoarse. "They will hand it over to Philip, who will rule Castilla in Juana's stead. Don Juan has devised a plot to align King Henry with Philip against your father."

I was dismayed by Don Rodrigo's words. "You speak of Don Juan Manuel. But what has this to do with Doña Elvira?"

"Everything, my lady. Doña Elvira also hates your father, and she has now found a way to use your desire to see your sister as a way to further her brother's plot. A meeting between Philip and King Henry could result in disaster for King Ferdinand and for Spain. Please, my lady princess," begged Don Rodrigo, "listen to me. Such a meeting must not take place. You must prevent it."

Was this another of his lies? Or was I finally hearing the truth? My thoughts raced in all directions. I was so shaken that I could barely stand. I needed to sit down, and I needed to think. "The chapel," I said. "Kindly accompany me there."

Somehow I managed to walk, unsteady as I felt, to the small chapel royal, the ambassador following at a little distance. Fortunately, the dimly lit chapel was empty, and we withdrew to a bench farthest from the altar. We spoke in whispers.

As the ambassador explained the situation in greater detail, I began to see how badly my mother had misjudged Doña Elvira. When I left Spain, my mother believed she had done me a great service by appointing Doña Elvira to stand in her stead as my protector and guide. Now I recognized that the lady's virtue was overshadowed by her thirst for power. This so-called virtuous woman was guilty of treachery—to me and to my father's kingdom. The betrayal was absolute. I felt my soul bleed. The time for weeping would come later.

All my life I had been schooled in obedience. As a result, I had obeyed Doña Elvira unquestioningly, even when I seethed with resentment. Now I could see that I had been wrong not to resist. Don Rodrigo must have understood all along that Doña Elvira was capable of plotting an intrigue against my father and the best interests of Spain. Now I chose to believe him.

When Don Rodrigo had answered all my questions, I told him to leave me. Alone, then, I walked with trembling legs to the front of the chapel, where I knelt before the altar and opened my aching heart to God's tender mercy. "Oh Lord," I prayed, "grant me the wisdom to see my duty and the strength to perform it." I have no notion of how long I remained there on my knees, but when at last I rose and made my way out of the chapel, I felt strong again.

My duty was clear now, and I acted without hesitation. I stormed into my duenna's chambers and confronted her. "I know that you are part of your brother's wicked plot to bring about the downfall of King Ferdinand."

Her already pallid face grew ashen, and her glittering eyes filled with fear. At first she attempted to deny any knowledge of a scheme or her complicity in any intrigue. But I would have none of her worthless denials.

"You are dismissed from my service, madam," I said, in a voice cold with fury. Doña Elvira dropped to her knees and waited with bowed head, for once unable to speak. "And you are no longer welcome here. I expect that you will leave England without delay."

I swept out of her chamber and assigned a servant to assist her—and to keep watch on her. Within three days she, her husband, and her son, Don Iñigo, were on a ship bound for Flanders.

My duenna was my duenna no more. Never again would she tell me what I could and could not do. Henceforth, I vowed, I would be mistress of my own court—and of my own life.

CHAPTER 12

Descent into Madness

Richmond Palace, November 1505

Prince Henry followed the page's smoking torch down a steep flight of rough stone steps to a dim cellar beneath the palace. A narrow, twisting passageway led to the heavy oak door of the alchemist's laboratory. The door swung open on creaking iron hinges. The king, wearing a leather apron over his rich garments, hunched over a table laden with mysterious instruments and vessels. Fumes filled the air. Henry breathed in the acrid stench. A strange feeling prickled Henry's skin. He believed that his father was actually capable of performing magic.

The king frequently called Henry to this secret laboratory to lecture him on his latest experiments.

Henry dreaded these lectures. The king had become more capricious; his irascibility increased, and his temper was often uncontrolled. He shouted at his servants, his gentlemen, his councillors, and especially his son. The older Henry got, the more he sensed his father's growing dislike of him. But why did the king dislike him? Henry did not know, but he suspected it was because his father wished that Arthur, the favorite, had lived, instead of Henry.

Henry watched silently as his father poured a murky liquid from one vessel into another.

For years King Henry had been searching for the secret of transmuting base metals into silver and gold. He was already wealthier than nearly all the rest of the English nobility put together. He owned many sumptuous palaces, old castles, manor houses, and hunting lodges, all of them repositories of his accumulated wealth—gold and silver plate, rich tapestries from the Netherlands, priceless ornaments from Italy, ironbound chests filled with gold. Buckingham often said that once a gold piece entered the royal coffers, it never came out again.

But even more important to King Henry than gold was the search for the elixir of youth—not to prolong his life forever, he had once explained to his son, but to become like a young man again. It was true that he looked like an old man: His once blond hair was now thin and gray, his body bent, his skin sallow, his teeth mostly blackened or missing. He believed he was on the verge of discovering the potion that would reverse all of this, and the belief kept him in his laboratory hour upon hour.

Absorbed in his experiments, the king seemed to forget

Henry. Time ticked by; Henry grew restless. Could he slip away unnoticed?

He would wait awhile longer. His father muttered to himself. An hour crawled by. Henry had challenged Brandon to wrestle this afternoon. He hoped Brandon would still be there. For some time now Brandon had become much taken up with the ladies of the court, and recently one of them had borne him a daughter. "So you are to be wed then?" Henry had asked when he heard the news. For a moment he thought of Princess Catherine with the shining auburn hair. But Brandon had shrugged off the question, remarking, "There are so many women to love!" He had winked at Henry and grinned knowingly. "As you shall soon discover, my lord."

Henry took a few quiet steps toward the door and pressed it until it opened slightly. As he pressed harder, the door creaked.

Alert as a deer, the king spun away from his array of instruments, glaring at the interruption. Henry froze, but it was too late. His father's wrath exploded.

"You have not been dismissed!" the king howled, seizing one of the glass vessels and hurling it at Henry, who tried not to flinch. The vessel missed Henry's head by a handspan and smashed against the stone wall. Maddened, the king hurled another vessel, and another while Henry, teeth clenched, disciplined himself to remain motionless. The inkhorn was the last to fly; ink trickled down the wall like blood.

"You may go," said the king, suddenly calm, apparently forgetting why he had summoned Henry in the first place, and Henry rushed away from the gloomy chamber.

When he found Brandon at last and they had stripped to their smallclothes, Henry rushed his opponent and threw him to the ground. Brandon fought back. He was six years older than the prince and had always defeated him easily. But Henry did not back down. Sweating and panting, the two struggled until Henry succeeded in pinning him. Henry stood over Brandon, grinning in triumph.

"The tide has turned," he said.

ONCE DOÑA ELVIRA HAD DEPARTED, I EXULTED IN AN unfamiliar sense of freedom. But I realized that to protect my reputation, I needed the presence in my household of an older, married lady. I thought of Lady Margaret Pole, who had become my friend at Ludlow and with whom I had since exchanged occasional letters. Unfortunately, her husband, Sir Richard, had recently died, and Lady Margaret herself was unwell. In any case, the decision was not mine but the king's. To spare himself the expense of a duenna, King Henry decided that I and my diminished court should take up residence at Richmond Palace as part of the royal household, where I would not require a governess.

At first I was pleased by this change, thinking it would give me opportunities to be with members of the English court and to see Prince Henry. I had only Puebla's word that the betrothal had been secretly renounced. Though he had been right about Doña Elvira, I still did not entirely trust the ambassador. If the betrothal had been broken, why had the king not told me? And if Henry and I were still betrothed, then why were marriage plans not going forward? I both hoped and dreaded that I might learn the answers if I lived under the king's roof.

Once ensconced at Richmond, though, I found that my freedom was more sharply curtailed than ever. I felt that members of the English court were watching me, whispering about me, speculating on my future. I was an outsider, a foreigner living in their midst, largely unwelcome. And I still spoke little English, barely enough to make my wishes known to the servants.

During those long, dreary days I thought often of my family. There were no letters from my father, and no money. My plan to meet with my sister, Juana, had come to nothing.

Then, seemingly by an act of God, my sister was brought to me, swept in by a great storm at sea.

In January of 1506, Juana's husband, Archduke Philip, made the foolhardy decision to sail from the Netherlands to Spain during a time of year known for its dangerous storms. Soon after their ships passed Calais, a violent gale battered them, scattering damaged vessels and terrified passengers along the southern coast of England.

Fortunately, my sister and brother-in-law and most of the others were rescued and brought ashore at Weymouth. When the news first reached me of the shipwreck and their narrow escape, the archduke was already being conducted to Windsor Castle, where King Henry planned to welcome them with great pomp and ceremony. I was invited to join them there.

Eager to spend time with my sister and to find out, if I could, what she might know of her husband's plans to seize power from our father, I made my way to

Windsor, accompanied by my ladies and gentlemen. There I learned that Juana had been left behind in Weymouth, "to recover from the frights of the voyage." Juana would join Philip when she felt well again.

Though I was disappointed that my sister was not present, I took part in the revelry, the tournaments and banquets, and the pageantry, determined to enjoy myself. I unpacked the gown I had ordered for Prince Henry's birthday celebration the summer before, and I dined and danced with my ladies in the Great Hall. Prince Henry was present, tall and very well made and increasingly handsome, his red-gold hair cut and combed straight in the French fashion. He thrilled the assembled company with his prowess in jousting and dancing. On two or three occasions when we were in sight of one another, I swept the prince a deep curtsy, and he bowed and smiled. But we did not exchange any words.

Despite my pleasure I also felt uneasy. King Henry and Archduke Philip disappeared together for long periods. Each time I saw them deep in conversation, my suspicions were aroused. What were they discussing in these private talks? Were they plotting the overthrow of my father while I danced?

On the day I was to return to Richmond with Princess Mary, my sister arrived at Windsor just as Philip announced that the ships were ready and they must prepare to sail while the weather held. In the end,

Juana and I had only two hours together, long enough for me to realize that this was not the sister I remembered. In place of the high-spirited and beautiful girl who had once laughed easily and loved to dance, I found a wan, silent woman, her lovely brown eyes brooding and fearful.

When I tried to embrace her, she shrank away from me. She strode about the chamber, wringing her hands, collapsing onto cushions, weeping, then struggling to her feet again to resume her pacing. I tried to distract her, but she would speak of nothing but her husband, Philip.

"I love him more than life itself, Catalina," she murmured. "But he loves me little. He has other women. He has not been faithful to his vows." Her voice rising, she began to rant about those who took her beloved Philip away from her—not only his numerous mistresses, but also his gentlemen with whom he liked to drink and hunt and disport himself. She was jealous of them all, even his hunting dogs—jealous to the point of madness.

"I am certain that Philip loves you, Juana," I said soothingly, though I was anything but certain.

Had we two sisters been able to spend more time together, perhaps we might have eventually found ourselves at ease with one another. I might have ventured to discuss my worries about our father and my own plight. Under the circumstances, I said nothing.

Our brief visit at an end, I kissed my sister, promising that we would surely meet again. I was disconsolate when she and her faithless husband left to sail away from the English port, for I feared that the archduke and the discontented Castilian noblemen would succeed in wresting control of the kingdom from my father, and I knew no way to prevent it.

The twenty-ninth of June, 1506, the day after Prince Henry's fifteenth birthday, by all rights should have been my wedding day, according to the terms of the marriage contract. Yet I had no idea when—or if!—the wedding would ever take place.

I did not even see Prince Henry on his birthday. In fact, I saw him rarely, though we lived in the same palace. My Spanish suite had been assigned to the poorest apartments, overlooking the courtyard where beggars congregated for handouts. That day I stood at my narrow window, gazing down at them in their rags and filth, women carrying hungry, wailing children on their bony hips, men kicking the starving dogs away from the meager portions thrown to the beggars from the royal kitchens. I felt like one of those ill-fed beggars, waiting for the king to toss me a crust. Meanwhile, elsewhere in the palace, Prince Henry's family and friends and the highest ranks of the nobility were celebrating the royal birthday.

I turned away from the window and looked to my ladies, observing their listless eyes and downcast expressions. They gazed at me impassively, awaiting my orders.

"Come with me," I told them, suddenly roused to anger. I picked up my skirts and hurried down the long gallery to the chamber of my household treasurer, Francesca, Inez, and Maria at my heels. Juan de Cuero looked up from his account books, startled to see us. It had been his custom to bring these records to my chamber each fortnight to show me the latest figures. Each time, my debts had increased.

"Don Juan," I said, "I am today ordering you to sell sufficient of my plate to give ten gold crowns to each member of my suite, to be spent as they wish."

The treasurer looked at me with eyes as wide and astonished as though I had ordered him to cut off his hand. "But, my lady princess, you know that I, as keeper of the plate, cannot—"

I slammed my fist on the account book. "Look at us, Don Juan! My ladies and I stand before you in rags and tatters, no better than the beggars in the courtyard! I order you to do so, do you understand, sir?"

He licked his lips and whispered, "It is a part of your dowry, madam."

"What good is my dowry to me? Tomorrow should be my wedding day. Perhaps the marriage contract no longer exists! In the meantime, we must eat, we must clothe ourselves, we must somehow continue to live! Now do as I have told you, good sir, with no further argument."

Cuero bowed his head. "As you wish, madam."

Piece by piece in the months that followed, one flagon, one ewer, one charger at a time, my dowry passed into the hands of the goldsmiths of London, who took advantage of my plight and offered only the most meager of returns for them.

Months passed with no change in my situation. Ambassador Puebla counseled patience once too often, until I lost not only my patience but my temper. "Don Rodrigo, do me a kindness: Do not return unless it is to bring me real news, and not merely idle gossip." I regretted my harsh words after I had dismissed him, but I did not call him back, and for some weeks he did not return.

Then, on a day in late November of 1506 when I had been brooding on the fact that I had now been in England for five years, Ambassador Puebla burst into my chambers. "I have news from Spain, and it is scarcely to be believed!" he exclaimed. "Archduke Philip is dead!"

Six months earlier, Philip and Juana had arrived in Spain. In October he fell ill, and in a matter of days he was dead.

"There is more," continued Don Rodrigo. "Queen Juana was profoundly shocked by the suddenness of the archduke's death. She grieved so deeply that she slept upon her knees by her husband's coffin and would not allow the corpse to be buried. She persuaded her loyal servants to seize the coffin from the monastery where it was being kept and to transport corpse and coffin all the way to Granada. The queen has said that at last she has her husband all to herself and will never again be parted from him."

She is mad, I thought. *My sister has truly gone mad.*

"But what of King Ferdinand?" I asked Puebla. "Cannot our father reason with her?"

"The king has her confined at the castle at Tordesillas," Puebla said. "He intends to rule Castilla in her stead."

I closed my eyes and murmured a brief prayer of thanks: Castilla and Aragon were still united, and my father held power. For that I was grateful, but naturally I added a prayer for the comfort of my poor, unfortunate sister.

The ambassador presented one more piece of news for which I was utterly unprepared: My father had married the niece of King Louis XII of France.

I gaped at Puebla. Had they all gone mad? "I knew nothing of this," I whispered.

"Her name is Germaine de Foix," said Puebla. "Your stepmother is just sixteen, of an age to bear him a male heir, if God wills it."

CHAPTER 13

Rebellion

Richmond Palace, April 1507

On the Feast of Saint George, Prince Henry rode into the lists upon a magnificent white gelding and easily unhorsed each of his opponents. Only Brandon presented a real challenge. At the banquets Henry played upon the virginals and accompanied himself with the lute as he sang songs of his own composition in a fine tenor voice. The ladies of the court blushed when he claimed them one by one as dancing partners. He could have had any of these ladies, he was well aware. The world was at his feet, his for the taking.

Or so it seemed. But in truth the prince still could not come and go as he pleased. To leave his apartments, he was forced to pass through his father's bedchamber. He took his meals alone but for two servitors and spent most of his time

*alone or with a few carefully selected companions—Bran-
don chief among them—or with his father, who was increasingly irrational and often violent.*

In recent days King Henry's fury seemed blunted. He
was less the wrathful warrior and more a weak and queru-
lous old man. He had not found the elixir of youth after all,
and he often spoke of the approaching end of his life and of
the splendid burial he planned. He had begun collecting
relics—fragments of the leg bone of Saint George, splinters
from the True Cross—to be made into part of the altar by
his tomb. He paid frequent visits to shrines around the
countryside and pledged to donate jeweled statues of himself, kneeling in prayer.

Yet even as the king contemplated his own death, he
was also weighing marriage to the newly widowed Queen
Juana of Castilla. "A fine wife she would make, the
beauty!" cackled the old king in Prince Henry's presence,
though court gossips whispered that she was quite mad.
"Whether or not she accepts my suit, I shall seek the betrothal of Princess Mary to Queen Juana's son, Charles.
And of you, Wales, to her daughter, Eleanor."

The king had mentioned other possible brides for the
prince of Wales: Marguerite d'Alençon of France was one;
the daughter of Duke Albert of Bavaria, another.

"What of Catherine of Aragon, my lord?" Henry asked.

"Not a possibility," said his father. "The political value
of the princess of Aragon has declined greatly since the death
of her mother. And her father's miserliness is intolerable."

Henry wondered if Catherine—Catalina, she once asked him to call her—was ever told that her betrothal had been broken nearly two years earlier. Surely the gossip had reached her. It was no secret that his father was considering other matches.

Henry had discussed the matter with Brandon. Now nearly sixteen, Prince Henry listened raptly to Brandon's tales of his amorous adventures. Brandon had somehow found a way out of his contract with Anne Browne, with whom he had a child, and was about to marry Anne's aunt, Lady Margaret Mortimer, a rich widow more than twice his age. "Marry for wealth and for advantage, my lord," Brandon advised. "Find love and take your pleasure where you will."

Henry pondered this advice. Was it not possible to do both—to marry for wealth and advantage, as his father insisted and Brandon agreed—and for love as well?

Henry pictured the fair-skinned Spanish girl with the intelligent gray eyes and the cascade of auburn hair. Months earlier the king had ordered Henry to have nothing to do with Princess Catherine. But the more his father forbade him to see Catherine or to speak to her, the more she was in his thoughts. He remembered the times they had spent together in the past, her lively mind, her gentle good humor. As he listened to Brandon's bragging tales of romantic conquest and of ladies who swooned for his attention, Henry thought always of Catherine. But he resolved that no matter what his father insisted, when the time came he would marry whom he pleased, whether his father was alive or dead.

By the spring of 1507 I was desperate. Unable to think of any other solution, I determined to see King Henry. One day when our larder was nearly empty, I dressed in a gown many times patched and mended, made my way through the palace to the royal apartments, and asked to speak with the king. Forced to wait for a lengthy time in his presence chamber, I endured the discomfiting stares of the courtiers who lounged about outside the king's chambers. No one spoke to me, and I imagined they were laughing behind my back.

Ushered at last into the king's privy chamber, I knelt three times, as required. The king glared at me. "What is it you want, madam?" he demanded.

"I have come to beg your help, Your Grace," I said, and described the straitened circumstances in which I found myself, unable even to properly feed my few servants. "Often, we have only spoiled fish and rotting vegetables and would go hungry were it not for the kindness of the duke of Buckingham who calls upon me from time to time with a gift of venison from his deer park."

The king peered at me from beneath craggy brows. I remembered the first time we had met, at Dogmersfield, and how King Henry had raised my veil and gazed at me with frank approval. Now he scowled. He saw me not as a lady in need of the assistance of the gallant knight he professed to be, but as a mere nuisance.

The king spoke. "You did not come naked from Spain, surely? You brought with you a goodly amount of plate and jewels, did you not, my lady Catherine?"

I agreed that I had.

"It is our understanding that upon the occasion of your marriage the plate and jewels became the property of your lawful husband, Arthur, prince of Wales. And upon the death of our beloved son Arthur, we became heir to all of his property, including the plate and jewels. Yet, you have continued to use this property, have you not, madam?"

I barely managed to stammer, "I have, Your Grace."

"And perhaps you have even sold several pieces for your own profit?" His eyes glittered cruelly. "Plundered the property of the Crown?"

I could scarcely believe what I heard: The king was accusing me of stealing! He smiled malignantly. I was trembling, but I willed strength to my limbs and steadiness to my voice. "I have sold only what is rightfully the property of the king of Spain, and only in time of dire necessity."

"We are under no obligation to provide further for you, madam," said the king coldly. "The prince of Wales repudiated the marriage agreement before his fourteenth birthday. Your support became entirely your father's duty, not ours. Anything we give you is merely

Christian alms. Be grateful for what you have." He turned away, waving his hand in dismissal.

So it was true! Henry had broken his promise to me!

"Such words are not worthy of Your Grace!" I cried. Nearly blinded by tears of humiliation, I made the necessary obeisances and fled from his chamber.

Soon after that dreadful scene I wrote to my father, congratulating him on his new marriage and describing what had happened. "If you have no money to spare from your treasury for me and my people," I wrote, "I entreat you, send me a new ambassador to replace Don Rodrigo, who is old and ill and unable to fulfill his duties. Send a gentleman who will truly be of assistance in dealing with the English king. Surely we are not meant to accept King Henry's statement that the prince of Wales has repudiated our agreement."

At the same time I wrote to the Observant Franciscans, the order to which my mother had been devoted, asking them to send a priest who could hear my confessions in Spanish, the language in which I prayed, the language of my heart.

Within a few months Fray Diego Fernandez, an intelligent, educated man of agreeable demeanor, arrived in my household. I immediately placed my trust in this devout man of the cloth with whom I also shared intellectual interests. The friar soon became my closest confidant, the only person on whose wisdom I believed I could completely rely.

Nevertheless, there were times when I felt that Fray Diego had in some ways taken the place of Doña Elvira. My duenna had assumed the duty of protecting my reputation. Fray Diego was concerned with protecting my soul. Soon after the friar's arrival Princess Mary invited me to travel with her for an event at court. Perhaps, I thought, this meant that I was still betrothed after all or might have the betrothal reinstated. But when I informed Fray Diego of my plans, the friar forbade me to attend. Asked the reason, he replied, "To avoid the appearance of sin, my child."

"What could possibly appear sinful when I am in the company of the king's daughter and her suite?" I protested.

"It is a mortal sin to take issue with your spiritual advisor, who sees more clearly than you the presence of evil," the friar reminded me sternly. "Is it not obvious that God has sent me to you, Lady Catalina, and that you must therefore be obedient to me in all things?"

And so I obeyed.

Months later my father wrote to me that a new ambassador was on his way to England, a nobleman named Gutierre Gomez de Fuensalida. My father assured me that Fuensalida would do everything necessary to soften the king in his treatment of me. And, best of all, Fuensalida was carrying with him the balance of my dowry, sixty-five thousand ducats, the coin of Aragon. I knew King Henry well enough to believe that with the rest of my dowry in hand he would surely reinstate my betrothal.

At last, I thought, with relief, *all will be well.* But I had thought that before, and I had been wrong.

Fuensalida arrived early in 1508 and took up residence at a mansion belonging to a wealthy Italian banker, Francesco Grimaldi. From the first, I found this aristocratic new ambassador haughty in demeanor. I soon realized he was arrogant, pompous, and humorless as well.

Ambassador Fuensalida took an immediate and intense dislike to Fray Diego, seldom missing an opportunity to slip some criticism of my confessor into our conversations. Fray Diego was much admired for his piety by the ladies of my court, and Fuensalida insinuated that the young friar was not above taking advantage of this. Fuensalida claimed that Fray Diego frequently exchanged the humble homespun robes of the Franciscans for the garments of a prosperous merchant and crept from the palace chapel to the dark passages of London where he indulged his weakness for drinking and fornication.

"The man is not fit to hear your confessions, my lady!" insisted Fuensalida. "He deserves to be removed from his position."

Nothing the ambassador said could have made me angrier. "What impertinence!" I cried. "What right have you to make such accusations?"

I had not thought there could be anyone less committed to my interests or more infuriating than Rodrigo Gonzales de Puebla, but alas, here he was!

My confessor and the new ambassador were not the only sources of strife in my little household. My ladies, who had been away from Spain for seven years, longed to return to their families. They were no longer the gay young maidens who had sailed from Spain believing they would find husbands at the English court. Maria de Salinas's former suitor had wed someone else after she was unable to provide a dowry. Her disappointment showed daily in her face, from which the fresh beauty had faded.

Maria and the others blamed Fray Diego for persuading me to remain in England in the hope of one day marrying Prince Henry, a hope my ladies saw as futile.

At least once a fortnight Francesca de Caceres, also dowerless, begged me to return to Spain. When I refused even to discuss the matter, she struck out at me angrily. "Catalina, why do you persist in your stubborn refusal to face the truth?" she cried, her face flushed. "You are no better off than any of us. King Henry will marry his son to the wealthiest daughter of the most powerful ruler he can find, and where will you be then? Let us return to Spain, where our families will provide for us, and we can hold up our heads with dignity!"

Stung by her words, I replied hotly, "How dare you speak to me in this manner! I am pledged to marry Prince Henry. My faith is in God that I shall one day reign as queen of this country. It is my duty to remain here. What do *you* understand of duty?"

After this heated exchange, Francesca, always one of my closest and most trusted friends, stopped pleading and turned to plotting. Through Fuensalida, she had made the acquaintance of his host, Signor Grimaldi. Without my knowledge, the increasingly rebellious and disloyal Francesca became a frequent visitor at the Grimaldi mansion. Soon the elderly banker made her an offer of marriage, and she accepted.

Francesca herself was too frightened or ashamed to tell me what she had done and sent Inez to break the news. "If she cannot go back to Spain," said Inez, "Francesca has made up her mind to marry the low-born Italian."

I was furious. Immediately I sent for Francesca, who stood before me, pale and quaking. "Ungrateful wretch!" I shouted. "How dare you betray me!"

Francesca threw herself at my feet. "I beg you, madam, forgive me. I have been so unhappy!"

"Duty must come before happiness, Francesca," I said coldly. "I forbid you ever to see Signor Grimaldi again. And I forbid you to have anything more to do with that deceitful ambassador who encouraged you in this scheme."

"As you wish, madam," Francesca whispered and fled from my presence without waiting for my dismissal.

Imagine then how shocked and horrified I was to learn that after our interview Francesca fled to her lover's house under cover of darkness. The next day, before I discovered her whereabouts, she married Grimaldi. Her treachery wounded me deeply, and I knew I could never forgive her.

It was simple to make out who was to blame for the dissatisfaction and intrigue that was growing like mold throughout my little court: Fuensalida.

By the autumn of 1508 I understood that the new ambassador himself had abandoned all hope of my marrying Prince Henry.

"Relations have worsened between England and Spain," said Fuensalida. "There is the grim possibility of war, and virtually no possibility of marriage."

"Can this be true?" I asked, deeply shaken by his words. "I had heard that King Henry wished to marry my sister and betroth his children to her children. And now he talks of war?"

The ambassador shrugged. "Political winds blow first one direction, then another."

Later I was appalled to discover that the ambassador had taken it upon himself, without consulting me, to have Grimaldi transfer my dowry money out of England for safe keeping. "Better than having the English seize it," he explained. "I was simply acting in your best interests, my lady princess. I have also taken the precaution of requesting a ship to take you and your suite away from this gloomy place forever, should the need arise."

I had given up years of my life to marry Prince Henry, and I was more determined than ever to be his wife and his queen. "I would rather die in England than go back to Spain without achieving my marriage," I told him. As soon as he had left my chambers I wrote the same sentiment to my father, adding, "Your ambassador here is a traitor. Recall him at once, and punish him as he deserves."

Most members of my household were openly rebellious, arguing among themselves but united in their desire to return to Spain, with my consent or without it. Princess Mary's ladies-in-waiting and the gentlemen of her suite blamed me for the delay of Mary's betrothal to my eight-year-old nephew, Charles, though I had nothing to do with the postponements. The king's mother, countess of Richmond and Derby, publicly ignored me, treating me as though I did not exist. It seemed I had no friends save Fray Diego.

Then Fuensalida informed me of the king's conclusion that a marriage between Henry and me was contrary to the Word of God. Members of the king's council were now asserting that my marriage to Arthur had been consummated: Arthur had boasted of it the morning after our wedding night, had he not? There were many who claimed to have heard him! Spots of blood were seen on the sheets! "A marriage between Prince Henry and his brother's widow would be a sin," the king insisted, apparently forgetting that two years earlier the pope himself had granted approval for the marriage.

As the year 1509 began, my life was in utter turmoil. Most of the silver and gold plate and all of my jewels had been sold at a great loss, simply in order to live. My treasurer, Juan de Cuero, boldly reproved me for using some of the money to buy books and other necessities for Fray Diego. Cuero sided with Fuensalida in his dislike of my confessor.

"You are no longer mistress of your own court, madam," Cuero said in one of several unpleasant conversations. "It seems that you have made Fray Diego Fernandez master over us all."

Stunned by his audacity, I replied angrily, "Perhaps, sir, the time has come at last for you to leave my service. I bid you a safe journey to Spain."

"As you wish, madam," said my treasurer, bowing, but not as low as he should have.

Soon many others of their own choice were packing for their journey back to Spain. Unfortunately, Fuensalida was not among them.

————

By the beginning of the Lenten season I had reached the lowest point of my life. Early one morning as I made my way to the chapel royal for mass, a mendicant dressed in tatters, his face hidden by a hood, stepped out of the shadows, begging for alms. I nearly passed by his pleas, for my own purse held only a few small coins of little value. The beggar followed after me, pleading, until I halted and gave him half of what I had. As I dropped the coins into his palm, I noticed that his hand was clean, white, smooth—not at all the hand of a beggar. During this exchange, he slipped a sealed letter from his sleeve into mine, murmured thanks, and slunk away.

The letter, whatever it was, seemed to burn through the cloth of my gown as I knelt through the long prayers, surrounded on every side by members of my court. When at last mass ended, I told my ladies that I wished to be left alone for a period of contemplation and quickly darted into a deserted alcove to read the letter. My hands were trembling as I broke the seal—the seal of the prince of Wales—and read the few lines written there in a graceful hand.

My dear lady princess Catalina: I have entrusted this letter to my loyal friend, Charles Brandon, who has come to you dressed in beggar's rags. Many times in the months past, forbidden by my father, the king, to be in your presence, I have wished to assure you that it is not I who is the cause of your distress. I know

no proper words with which to continue this letter
other than to say that I am your obedient servant,
Henry, prince of Wales.

I read the letter several times over, kissed it, and placed it in my prayer book for safe keeping. I did not know what it meant, or if anything in my life would change. But at least I had a glimmer of hope, and one in which I trusted.

The entire court watched as King Henry's health declined through the weeks of spring. He proclaimed the customary pardon for criminals. He stopped appearing at court, and his physicians reported that he was coughing up blood. When he did not leave his bedchamber, we knew that death was drawing nigh.

Prince Henry would soon become the new king. My future depended upon him. I reread his brief letter and told myself that Henry cared for me. Perhaps he even loved me as a brother loves his dear sister. But did he wish to have me as his wife? Or would he choose someone else?

I alone clung to the belief that Prince Henry would choose to marry *me*. I could not allow myself to believe otherwise.

CHAPTER 14

The Broken Spell

Richmond Palace, April 1509

Prince Henry knelt by his father's bedside, at times praying, at times simply holding the sick man's bony hand. The king's cheeks were sunken, his eyes hollow, as though his face were already a death mask.

The royal bedchamber was crowded with physicians and astrologers, priests and courtiers, their eyes fixed upon the king, ears straining for any last words from the dying monarch. They heard only the rattling cough, the strangled gasps.

For twenty-four hours Henry watched the king's labored breathing, the tortured chest rising and falling in the struggle against the sharp assaults of death. His father had not spoken for some time. Knowing that it would soon be over, Henry wished now that he and his father had not ex-changed so many harsh words, had not allowed disagree-ments to turn into bitter arguments. Soon enough the old king's final fight would end, and young Henry would be-come the new king. His father was leaving him a peaceful kingdom, enormous power, and untold wealth.

The king's lips quivered and his eyelids fluttered open. The gray eyes stared at Prince Henry. Did his father recog-nize him?

"Send them away," the king whispered.

The prince turned to face those who crowded into the bedchamber. "Leave us!" he said in his most commanding tone. "The king wishes it."

They shuffled reluctantly toward the door, afraid of missing the moment at which the king's breath expired and his spirit departed his body. The door closed, and Prince Henry was alone with his father. The king worked to form words. Henry placed his ear close to the lips of the dying man. "What is it, my lord? Tell me."

"Marry her," he whispered.

"Marry whom?" asked the prince. "Whom should I make my wife?"

"You—know—who—" gasped the king. A ghost of a smile passed his lips.

These were his last words. The struggle was over. Prince Henry was free.

ORD OF THE KING'S DEATH SPREAD QUICKLY DURING the early morning hours of the twenty-first of April. I heard the slow, mournful tolling of bells and immediately understood their meaning. I dressed quickly in my black gown, summoned Maria and Inez, and hurried to the chapel royal where prayers for the dead were already being chanted.

Head bowed and hands folded in prayer, I glanced around furtively for some sign of Henry. Presently he entered the chapel, his grandmother leaning on his arm. The frail old countess appeared almost joyful, radiant in the knowledge that her only child had taken his place among the angels.

I confess that I found no tears to shed for the dead king, who had made my past seven years a misery. Still, I prayed for God's mercy upon his wretched soul.

I was keenly aware of the covert glances of others as I left the chapel royal and returned to my chambers, accompanied by Fray Diego and my ladies. I had scarcely removed my veil when there was a knock at the door and a page's voice rang out, "Announcing His Highness, King Henry the Eighth!"

For a moment I was too surprised to act. My ladies' eyes grew large with wonder. My confessor frowned.

The knock and the announcement were repeated.

My heart beating erratically, I collected my wits, stepped to the door, and opened it myself.

Robed in mourning garments that were nonetheless richly furred and trimmed in jewels, the young king filled the doorway with his splendor. "You are dismissed," he said. His words were addressed to my attendants, but his blue eyes were fixed upon mine. Fray Diego and my ladies threw me furtive looks and hurried away. I was alone with the new King Henry.

Keenly aware of my well-worn gown—the "new" gown that was no longer new—I swept him a deep curtsy. "Your Grace," I murmured, my eyes lowered, my gaze fixed upon his velvet slippers.

"Catalina," he said softly.

When I dared to raise my eyes, he was smiling. "Yes, my lord," I replied, taking the hand he offered and hoping that he could not detect the trembling in mine.

"It would please me greatly if you would consent to be my wife," he said gravely.

Happiness squeezed the breath from my chest, and tears of joy threatened to overflow. But I met his eyes and said more calmly than I felt, "I consent, my lord, with all my heart."

Henry dropped to his knees. "Catalina," he said earnestly, his eyes moist and shining, "I do solemnly pledge to you my love and my loyalty, unto death." With these words he slipped a magnificent ruby ring upon my finger and pressed his lips upon my hand.

The king rose to his feet—how tall he was!—and soon he was gone, leaving me standing there, giddy with delight. *I have done it!*

Before I called my ladies to tell them the news, I seized parchment and quill and dashed off a short note to my father: *The game is ours.* With the help of God, I had persevered through seven long years of tribulation, and I had won! The evil spell under which I had lived for so long had at last been broken.

There was much to be accomplished in the weeks that followed. Henry relied upon me to help him with plans for his father's funeral. As it became obvious that I was the new king's chosen bride, people at court who had ignored me or insulted me over the years were suddenly treating me with the kind of deference I had deserved all along. And I did revel in that!

Perhaps the most disconcerted by this sudden turn of events was Fuensalida. My relationship with the ambassador had become badly strained, and when he requested an audience I granted it reluctantly. So certain had he been that the new king would wed someone else that he now seemed almost in a daze. In no mood to punish anyone, I accepted his explanation that he had only wished to help me.

For a fortnight the old king's body lay in state in the Great Hall of Richmond Palace. It made its final earthly journey on the tenth of May, when the coffin was carried in solemn procession to Westminster Abbey. Following the requiem mass, the body of King Henry VII was laid to rest next to Queen Elizabeth's in the vault beneath the unfinished chapel he had recently ordered built.

Into the hushed gloom of the abbey, crowded with noble families from every part of the kingdom, strode a herald of the Knights of the Bath. "Long live Henry the Eighth, king of England!" cried the herald, and the company responded with a ringing shout, "Long live Henry the Eighth, king of England!" My voice, choked with emotion, joined the others: "Long live Henry the Eighth, king of England!"

One era had ended and another begun for England, and for me as well.

Henry set the date of his coronation for Midsummer Day, the twenty-fourth of June, only six weeks after the funeral. I was moved with my little suite to chambers at Richmond more fitting for the future queen. Henry fell into the comfortable habit of coming by to visit me unannounced nearly every day. He always insisted that we speak in private. Fray Diego disapproved—to meet with my future husband without the presence of my confessor was a sin. I ignored him. Then the friar voiced a far greater objection.

"It is my religious duty, madam, to warn you: This marriage does not conform to the laws of the church.

Divine scripture puts forth in the twentieth chapter of Leviticus, 'If a man shall take his brother's wife, it is an unclean thing: He hath uncovered his brother's nakedness; they shall bear their sin; they shall die childless.'"

A chill ran through me, but I shook it off. "Pope Julius granted a dispensation. The marriage was not consummated. I am still pure."

The friar continued as though I had not spoken. "I believe that the dispensation was granted in error, and that this new marriage will not be valid. A mortal sin, my lady."

It was the final straw! I made up my mind to have no more of Fray Diego's interference.

"You have been my confessor for two years, good friar," I said. "And I look forward to maintaining that relationship in the years to come. But I no longer need you to advise me on what is a sin and what is not. When in future I desire your advice, I shall ask for it."

The friar's lips were set in an unyielding line as he saw his authority over me slipping away. But I was mistress now, and I found it remarkably easy to assert my new power though not so easy to forget his words: *This marriage will not be valid.*

I turned my attention to my little court. Henry had sent me a generous gift of money, and from this treasury I gave sums to those loyal retainers who had remained with me during the long years of misery and uncertainty. Next, I called to my service an old friend, Lady Margaret Pole. I had not seen her since my departure from Ludlow, though we had exchanged occasional letters and I knew of the death of her husband and the straitened circumstances in which the widow found herself. Our reunion was bittersweet, both of us shedding tears.

When we were seated, I called for spiced wine. Servants appeared with platters of confits, to which we helped ourselves. I marveled—it had been far too long since I had had such treats served in my own apartments.

"Eight years ago I left my home in Spain," I reminded my friend, "and I have had just one new gown in all that time!" That gown—ordered for Henry's fourteenth birthday celebration, to which I was then not invited—was now so badly worn that I had called upon Buckingham's sister to lend me something to wear to the old king's funeral. "I need new gowns, robes, chemises, shifts, kirtles, petticoats, slippers, everything! I scarcely know where to begin, Lady Margaret. Can you help me find silkwomen, embroiderers, seamstresses, glove makers, and furriers?"

Lady Margaret beamed at me fondly. "And a wedding gown, my lady? Should that not be in the plans as well?"

I felt myself blush. "Yes, that too," I agreed, fingering the diamond pendant I now wore. Nearly every day a new jewel arrived from the royal treasury, sent by Henry.

We planned to be married secretly, well before the coronation, for the king wanted me by his side, crowned when he was crowned. I said no more, but Lady Margaret smiled knowingly. "It is well to be prepared," she said, her fine brows arched, and I agreed.

On the tenth of June Henry and I boarded the royal barge at Richmond. Under a sky as blue as any I remembered in Spain, we swept beneath London Bridge on the sparkling surface of the Thames. The white carpet of swans parted for us. I had made this river journey several times, but never had my heart been so filled with joy. Minstrels played for our pleasure, and Henry borrowed a lute and sang for me one of the little Spanish songs I had taught him when he was still a boy. Listening to his sweet voice, the years between then and now fell away, and my heart lifted and sang with his.

At Greenwich, I was escorted to the queen's apartments, where I dined alone, attended by a few servitors. Early the next morning, after matins and a breakfast I was far too nervous to eat, my maidservants dressed me in a simple gown of pure white silk that opened upon a white petticoat trimmed in gold lace.

My bridegroom arrived in a suit of white velvet and led me out of the palace and into the morning sunshine. We walked solemnly—though I felt like dancing!—to the chapel of the Observant Friars by the palace walls, where the archbishop of Canterbury, William Warham, awaited our arrival.

There were no banquets after the ceremony, though we both took pleasure in feasting and dancing, and no jousting, though Henry enjoyed the tiltyards more than any other place. And—thanks be to God!—there was no official bedding ceremony, no blessing of the matrimonial chamber, only the complete privacy we both desired.

That night we became not only man and wife, but lovers. Henry found me a maiden untouched.

And thus began our married life.

Within days word began to spread of our marriage, and I found to my delight that everyone I encountered seemed as pleased as I that the wedding had taken place at last.

According to custom, on the night before our coronation my husband (how I loved to say those words: *my husband*) and I slept at the ancient Tower of London. The next morning, to the joyous pealing of bells from every belfry in the city, we made our way to Westminster Abbey. My white satin gown set off to advantage my auburn hair that fell nearly to my waist. Bedecked in many of the jewels Henry had given me, I rode in a litter between two palfreys who were trapped to the ground in gorgeous brocades. I was surrounded by ladies of the court dressed in cloth of gold and silver or in brightly colored velvets.

Exuberantly cheering throngs of simple folk crowded the narrow streets. Members of the artisans' guilds stood rank upon rank. Clergymen of every church and chapel were arrayed in their finest copes, their jeweled crosses carried before them.

The greatest cheers went up for the handsome young king dressed in robes of scarlet velvet furred with ermine. His doublet of gold was adorned with diamonds and other precious stones, and across his chest he wore a baldric set with enormous rubies.

"Long live King Henry the Eighth!" shouted the people until they must have been hoarse. "Long live Queen Catherine!"

I turned to Lady Margaret Pole, who rode beside me. "I have another favor to ask of you, dear friend," I said.

"Only ask it, my lady."

"Please," I said, "will you teach me to speak English?"

The ceremonies went on for many hours. The celebrations that followed would have continued for many days, had it not been for the death of the king's grandmother, the countess of Richmond and Derby, reminding us of the fate that awaits us all.

The months of summer were without doubt the happiest of my life. After years of being kept in seclusion by the will of our fathers, Henry and I gave ourselves up to pleasure. We hunted together, ate and drank together, danced together, and at night retired to our blissful bed.

By the first cool days of autumn, I knew that I was with child. My cup of happiness was overflowing. Henry and I prayed fervently for the birth of a son to become England's next king. That would make our joy complete.

EPILOGUE

Buckden Towers, Huntingdonshire, England
December 1533

THE POUNDING AT MY DOOR HAS RESUMED. CHARLES Brandon, duke of Suffolk, has returned, shouting more threats to drag me away, promising that worse is yet to come. I refuse to answer him. Elsewhere in the castle a horrific racket is taking place, as though it were under siege. I ignore it. Brandon's men have packed up nearly everything that can be moved—beds, tables, tapestries. From my latticed window I watch as carts and men slink away.

For now, at least, Brandon has given up.

The country folk, assured that I am safe when I wave to them, are slowly returning to their cottages, leaving behind their humble gifts of bread and cheese and preserved meat.

There is much more to my story of the twenty-four years of marriage to King Henry, the great love of my life, a marriage that Henry has declared at an end. I am weary now, and in need of rest. There are others who will continue my story.

I have not relented, and I shall not. I have not submitted, and I shall not. Brandon has given up, but I know that the king has not. I am stubborn not for my own sake, but for the sake of my daughter, Mary, who shall, if there be a just God, one day rule this country as its rightful queen. I sign this

Catherine, the Queen
31 December 1533

HISTORICAL NOTE

CATHERINE OF ARAGON HAD ENDURED AND WON. HER
next test of endurance and courage was her duty—and
desire—to provide Henry and the realm with a male
heir.

Catherine's first pregnancy, coming soon after her
wedding and coronation, ended before its time in the
stillbirth of a daughter. She had barely recovered when
she became pregnant once again. On the first of December 1510, she made her formal withdrawal from
court. Following detailed instructions laid down years
before by the countess of Richmond and Derby for
Henry's mother, Elizabeth of York, Catherine remained
secluded with her ladies in a darkened chamber hung

with tapestries that covered the windows and doors, as well as walls and ceilings.

Soon after midnight on New Year's Day of 1511 she gave birth to a fine, healthy boy. Henry came to her with his eyes shining with love and pride, and all of England celebrated the birth of a prince. But joy was brief. While the royal couple and their court were at Westminster in February, word came from Richmond that the infant had sickened and died. For months Catherine remained withdrawn in a somber state, praying, fasting, and weeping.

This dark time became even darker when Catherine learned that her husband had taken a mistress. Her love for him had grown and deepened during their two years of marriage, and though he showed her great respect, seeking her company and her counsel, it was plain that his ardor had cooled. But Henry continued to visit Catherine's bed in an effort to produce a son. Time after time she conceived; time after time she miscarried or the infant was stillborn. Then, on the eighteenth of February, 1516, in the seventh year of marriage, Catherine delivered a healthy, living child—a daughter. They named her Mary, and though they rejoiced in her birth, Mary could not fill the need for a male heir.

For Catherine, there were no more live births. For Henry, there was a new mistress: Elizabeth Blount. In 1519 she bore him a son whom he named Henry, adding Fitzroy—"the king's son." The humiliation was almost more than Catherine could bear, yet she dutifully attended the celebration at which King Henry presented his bastard child to the court. The infant was provided with a complete household, befitting the son of a king.

Catherine forgave Henry, but she would not forgive him passing over their daughter, Mary, princess of Wales, to give his bastard son a string of royal titles, as though *he* were heir to the throne. When Catherine objected, the king punished her by taking away three of her Spanish ladies-in-waiting.

In the winter of 1521 Catherine again lost a stillborn child and knew this would be her last pregnancy. That was the first time she heard Henry say: "Perhaps it is as the Scriptures said—our marriage is sinful, and we are condemned to die without sons."

There were more mistresses, many of them ladies of Catherine's court. Most came and went in a matter of weeks as the king's interest moved restlessly from one to the next, lighting at last upon Mary Boleyn, who was, in time, replaced by her younger sister, Anne Boleyn, a woman of dark looks, biting wit, flirtatious manner, and unequalled ambition.

Anne joined Catherine's court in 1522, when she returned from France and the court of King Francis. Catherine watched their flirtation with as much patience as she could muster. Five years later Henry informed Catherine that their marriage was at an end, and that he intended to divorce her to marry Anne.

"The marriage never was," he said. "Our union was based on a misunderstanding of Scripture. It is an abomination in the sight of God! As a matter of conscience, we must divorce."

For more than six years Catherine continued to insist that she was the king's legal wife, her previous marriage to Arthur was unconsummated, and there were no grounds for divorce. Through Henry's petitions to Rome, his appeals to the intellectuals of Europe, and his attempts to intimidate and humiliate her, Catherine stood firm.

Finally Henry ordered Catherine to leave Greenwich Palace for Richmond. There were subsequent moves, each to a lodging more isolated and uncomfortable than the one before. From these remote places, Queen Catherine learned of the annulment of her marriage, the king's marriage to Anne Boleyn, and Anne's coronation with her great pregnant belly showing beneath her robes. In July of 1533, Henry ordered Catherine to move once more, this time to Buckden. Along the way well-wishers lined the road, cheering and calling out their support. In her more than twenty years as their queen, Catherine had become much beloved of the people, and the outpourings of loyalty and devotion touched her deeply, angering the warders who accompanied her.

Queen Catherine was later moved one last time, from Buckden to Kimbolton Castle, another dank and unhealthful place. There were numerous attempts to frighten her, threatening her and her daughter with martyrdom if she refused to acknowledge Anne Boleyn as rightful queen. Catherine resolved to go to her death willingly, if that was to be her fate.

Catherine's health deteriorated. On January 7, 1536, she died without having yielded to the king's demands that she renounce her title as queen. Some suspected that she might have been subjected to a slow poison, but these suspicions went unproven.

King Henry's marriage to Anne Boleyn produced one child, Elizabeth, and ended with Anne's execution, ordered by the king himself, only five months after Catherine's death. King Henry married four more times before his death on January 28, 1547. He was succeeded as king by Edward, his son by his third wife, Jane Seymour. When Edward died in 1553, Princess Mary, daughter of Catherine of Aragon, was crowned queen.